DEADLOCK

A DARCIE LOCK ADVENTURE

JULIA GOLDING

For Emily and Florence
And thanks to John Dickinson for identifying the perfect recruit
for SIS

Frost Wolf

First published 2011
by Frost Wolf
www.juliagolding.co.uk

ISBN 978-0-9570539-8-4

Cornwall, England: Sunny spells, 17°C

Marcus Galt stared at the carnage in disbelief. As he turned his head to take in the full extent of the damage, his long grey plait writhed on the back of his jacket like an angry snake. He clenched the top of the tube-shaped weapon he held across his chest, grinding his thick-soled black boots into the mud.

'That's it! I've had it up to here with them.' He chopped at his throat. 'They've totally devastated everything. They've got to die!'

His partner, a willowy woman in her early sixties,

stood beside him, blonde hair threaded with white but worn long like a girl. Her hand fluttered to his arm, appealing for mercy, as her tie-dye scarves flapped in the breeze.

'Isn't that a bit cruel, my love?' she asked.

'It's no more than they deserve.' Marcus's face was set behind his steel-rimmed glasses. 'The stuff's ready now – been brewing long enough. We have enough to wipe them all out. It's my secret weapon of mass destruction.'

'But, Marcus –'

'By tonight, there won't be a single one left alive. What do you think of that, eh, Darcie?'

Marcus Galt raised his voice to snag the attention of their guest who was in the bean patch, half hidden behind the shed. Darcie stood up and stretched – her back was killing her from all the hard work they had put her to since her arrival.

'Yeah, go for it,' Darcie said, slicking back her black fringe as it tumbled into her eyes.

'Good girl. Got more gumption than you, Claire.' Marcus unscrewed the top of the plastic bottle and tipped. A pale brown liquid glugged into a shallow tub set into the soil. 'Anyway, it's all organic. Bye bye, slugs. Die happy in my homebrew,' the gardener chanted vindictively, nudging one over the edge into the liquid.

Job done, Marcus took a swig from the bottle for himself and returned to digging his row of potatoes.

Darcie watched him for a moment, but when he didn't explain, decided she had to ask.

'Mr Galt –?'

'Marcus, love, Marcus.'

'Erm, Marcus, what's with the beer?'

'The slugs have been ruining my brassicas. They sniff out the homebrew and drink themselves to death. Not a bad way to go.'

Pondering this strange form of chemical warfare, Darcie put down the full basket of runner beans and sat on the step by the shed. She poured herself a coffee from the thermos flask and nibbled on one of Claire's wholemeal biscuits. She was starving. Since arriving in the dead of night at Mr and Mrs Galt's house a week ago, she had spent most of the daylight hours with them on their allotment on the edge of Truro, a pretty cathedral city in the far south-west of England. It had been a surreal experience: at one moment, she was in Egypt, running from the American president, her escape masterminded by her friend Stingo, an SAS officer; next she was in a green corner of the English countryside where the biggest enemy were slugs. She remembered asking Stingo to find her a quiet, sunny beach to lie on until her problem with President Morris blew over; he'd brought her here, to get a tan while picking beans with his parents.

'Truro, no safer place,' he'd told her. Beaches only a few miles away. And she'd be back home in England where it would be easier to protect her from her enemies.

Perhaps he was right – though to be honest, England felt a foreign country to Darcie, who had spent most of her life abroad. But it was as good a place as any to go to ground because, even if the president stopped chasing her, there was still the little matter of a grudge borne her by Madame Tsui, head of an organised crime syndicate in the Far East. It was more than enough powerful enemies for one fourteen-year-old schoolgirl to have made in the last few months.

But then, Darcie Lock's life had stopped being ordinary when she first learned that her parents were spies. Michael Lock was a British Secret Intelligence Service agent; her mother, Ginnie, a CIA operative. Darcie had been sucked into their life of espionage and couldn't seem to find a way out.

In Truro, she was trying her hardest to escape the

octopus grip of the secret services. Cut off from contact with her parents for the time being, holidaying in a place well off everyone's radar screen, she might be able to claw back some normality for herself. It was a strange, hangover-from-the-hippy-sixties normality with the Galts, but it was safe. No one was shooting at her, trying to blow her up, or leaving her pegged out in a desert to die. Safe.

'Well, well, look who it is!' exclaimed Claire, shading her eyes as she gazed down the slope to the road. Beyond the boundary of the allotments, the spike of the cathedral spire shot up from the bottom of the valley like one of Marcus's cabbages that had gone to seed, towering over the other buildings. Much closer, walking briskly up the cinder path towards them, was Stingo.

'Hardly ever get a visit from him and now he comes twice in ten days,' muttered Marcus, digging his spade into the soil to leave it standing.

'Darling, this is unexpected!' exclaimed Claire, wiping her hands on her patchwork apron and moving down the path to hug her son. 'Everything all right?'

'Hi, Mum.' Stingo returned her embrace before letting go. He ran his hand briefly over his short sandy crop as if suddenly reminded of how different he was from his long-haired parents. Stingo was about Claire's height but at least twice her bulk, thanks to the serious physical training he did each day. 'Yeah, everything's fine. How's things? Is she behaving?' His pale blue eyes flicked towards Darcie, already smiling.

'She's been an angel.' Claire beamed at her guest.

'Of course I'm behaving,' said Darcie, returning Stingo's hug. 'They've survived having you in the house as a teenager; I must be a dream.'

Darcie was so excited to see him, having felt completely out of the picture for the past few days. He'd know where her parents were – how President Morris had reacted to her disappearance – where she was going next.

Stingo reached out a hand to his father. 'Dad.'

'Kennedy.'

Kennedy? What kind of a name was that, wondered Darcie as the two men shook hands stiffly. No wonder he used a nickname.

'I hope you're staying for lunch, darling?' asked Claire.

'Yeah, if you've enough. I promised Darcie a beach so I thought I'd take her surfing this afternoon.'

'Great!' Darcie smiled broadly at him, feeling the

day was definitely looking up – anything was better than an afternoon of gardening chores among the drowning slugs.

'Thought we'd hit the north coast – the surf's up and some of my squad will be there. They're sorting you out a board and a wetsuit.'

'Fantastic!' She could think of nothing better than spending time with Stingo and the other SAS men; they worked hard but really knew how to play when they had a chance.

'We're already taking bets on how long you'll last.'

She punched him in the ribs. 'Longer than you. I've got pretty good balance.'

'OK, I'll take that bet.'

'What do I get when I win?'

'When?! Prepare to be humiliated, Darcie. Ready to put your money where your mouth is?'

'Kennedy!' his father said reprovingly.

'Er, you get the glory, of course. Couldn't possibly encourage a teenager to place money on a bet, could I?' Stingo said with false innocence as he winked at her behind his father's back. Being with his parents was making his mischievous side emerge.

Lunch was vegetarian pâté sandwiches, celery sticks and carrot cake, eaten on a picnic blanket on a grassy patch in front of the shed. Stingo's parents kept pressing him for personal stuff – information about his girlfriends, career, what he did with his free time – but he avoided answering them with expert diversionary tactics. Darcie enjoyed following the game, picking up tips for when she next saw her own parents. When Claire asked if he was still seeing 'that nice Italian girl', he asked about progress on her quilting. When Marcus began to express loud views as to the war on terror and role of the Special Forces therein, Stingo turned the subject to the ongoing battle his dad was having with the neighbour on the next allotment over the use of pesticides.

The question Stingo couldn't dodge was the one to which he knew he owed his parents an answer. Taking advantage of the opportunity presented by Darcie going off to take the picnic basket back to the car, Claire Galt jumped in with the subject they had been saving up all week.

'If you don't mind me asking, darling, how do you know Darcie, exactly? You said she was in trouble – I know we spoke to her parents on the phone about having her to stay for a while – but can't you explain some of it to us? We're dying of curiosity.'

'She's done nothing wrong,' Stingo said quickly, wondering how much he could tell them. They all watched Darcie walk down to the Galts' cranky old car, her long black hair bobbing in a high ponytail. Tall for her age, she moved with the rangy pace of an athlete.

'Of course not. She's a sweet girl, we know that. But still . . .'

'I met her on a personal protection assignment in Africa. She got involved in something dangerous thanks to . . . well, let's say her parents don't stack shelves in the supermarket for a living.' He decided not to mention the Egyptian angle: his parents were bound to have followed the Shelly Morris kidnap on the news and would guess too much. 'She needs to stay somewhere for a while until things die down. In fact, I was going to ask you a favour: can she stay a bit longer?'

Claire glanced at Marcus. 'As long as she needs, darling.'

'I can't pretend that there'll be no danger if we're really unlucky and the people after her catch up with her whereabouts. It shouldn't happen – but I can't promise it won't.'

'Even more reason for her to stay,' said Marcus

gruffly, fiddling with the gold hoop he wore in one ear. 'Sounds like she needs some friends.'

'Thanks.' Stingo met his father's eyes. 'You know, Dad, when I was going out on a limb to help Darcie a few weeks back, I thought of you.' He looked down. 'I thought it's the one thing I've done you'd be proud of.'

Marcus cleared his throat. 'But I am proud of you, Kennedy: I may not agree, but I've always been proud. I respect you for doing what you think is right. We'll take care of her for you and her parents, don't you worry.'

Darcie was unaware that she'd been the catalyst for something of a family reconciliation when she returned, but she could feel the warmth in the family group and see the smiles. Stingo looked much younger than normal, squatting alongside his dad as they discussed the cricket. The tough-nut warrant officer had cracked to reveal the sweet fact that he was somebody's son. It was good to have him around: Marcus and Claire were nice enough, but they were a bit odd and knew nothing about who she really was. Stingo was her only connection to her real life with her parents. Perhaps he'd come to say they'd found a way to get her out of hiding?

'So, Darcie, how do you fancy going to school in Truro?' Stingo asked.

Darcie felt a swoop of disappointment in her stomach like missing a step in the dark. It seemed as if she was going nowhere fast. 'What, here?'

'Yeah. Schools go back next week. Your parents want your nose to the grindstone, studying for your GCSEs. They've sorted it out through their own channels and picked a school for you. Enrolled you as Darcie Galt.' He gave her a wry smile. 'We'll pretend you're my cousin.'

Annoyed with her parents now, Darcie wondered why they hadn't asked her first, instead of sending Stingo to do their dirty work. 'So what you're really saying is that it's all sorted and I don't have a choice?'

'Don't blame your mum and dad,' said Stingo, 'they're out of it at the moment. Your mum's been hauled back to Washington – she's getting a lot of hassle.'

Darcie scowled. It wasn't difficult to work out who was giving her mother a hard time. Ginnie's chief would be down on her hard, trying to find out where she'd hidden her daughter. In most cases when someone at work gets at you, there is a boss higher up to whom you can appeal; the problem for

Ginnie was that her chief was the president of the United States and you can go no higher than that. He was on the campaign trail and was worried that if it came out he had sanctioned the use of a child to spy on his own daughter, it would ruin his chance of re-election. He wanted to tuck Darcie away somewhere until the danger of a media backlash passed, but there was no guarantee when that would be.

'You should cut your parents some slack,' Stingo continued. 'This isn't easy for them either.'

Darcie crumbled the remainders of her bit of cake so that it fell between her fingers. 'OK. Fine. Whatever.'

Stingo rolled his eyes. 'Well, that's a really mature response, Darcie, after everyone's gone to so much trouble for you.'

'Who are you now, Stingo: my dad? 'Cause you sound a lot like him.' Darcie jumped up to walk off her frustration. Stingo watched her stalk away, his brow creased.

Claire reached out and patted her son's hand. 'She's right, you know. You were being too tough on her considering you'd just delivered bad news. I think she was hoping you were going to take her home.'

Marcus chuckled. 'I never thought I'd see the day when my son turns into an old nag.'

Stingo's face cracked into a smile. 'Teenagers!' he said with an exaggerated sigh. 'Bet I was never like that.'

'You were just like that, Kennedy,' said Claire with a fond smile. 'Exactly like that.'

Nairobi, Kenya: Hot and dry, 30°C

Hugo Kraus stared at the metal door to his cell, counting the rivets. He knew how many there were already: thirty-four. He'd been counting them every hour of every day since he was put in jail four months ago to slow cook in this airless cell. On his rare visits to the other side, he was surrounded by yet more doors of the same kind. He counted every one of them when he had a chance and they all had the same number of rivets.

'Control, Hugo, control,' he muttered, screwing down his anger.

Inside though, he was screaming with rage and hate. They'd thrown him in this stinking prison and chucked away the key. He was only freaking seventeen – he couldn't spend his life like this! He understood his crime: he'd been involved in a plot to overthrow the Kenyan president. Sure, people would get mad at him, but it wasn't his fault! No, it was the fault of his father and all the other morons who had mucked up big time. He fumed, his dark mood building like a geyser erupting in scalding water. It was no comfort that his father was also enjoying Kenyan prison hospitality in a worse place than this – youth had at least earned Hugo a cell to himself while they assessed his mental stability. The geek doctor thought he was mad – and so he was: mad as hell at those who'd let him down.

His thoughts turned to Darcie Lock as they always did at this point, like a Grand Prix driver rounding the same corner in yet another high-speed lap of hate. If the girl hadn't got in the way, none of this would've happened. He could have been enjoying the good life – not sweating in this pigpen.

He passed a few pleasurable moments imagining what he would do to her if their paths ever crossed again. She'd humiliated him – beaten him. No one ever beat Hugo Kraus and got away with it. Next time their roles would be reversed and he would savour every moment of the victory. He glossed over the fact that she had acted in self-defence when he'd tried to kill her, choosing to remember Darcie as the intruder, he as the defender of his father's plot. Yeah, she was to blame.

There was a scrape at the door as the key turned in the lock. Hugo tensed on his bed, ready to spring up. If it was the quack again, he didn't want to seem weak. He was a soldier, a prisoner of war, not a nutcase. But when the door swung open, two strangers stepped inside – a young man accompanied by a short, non-descript old woman.

'Mr Kraus?' asked the man. He had limp brown hair and fiddled nervously with a blue file he was carrying. Obviously a weakling.

'What do you want?'

'I'm Bernard Jenkins from the British High Commission.'

'So?'

'You've got dual nationality, I believe?'

'I'm Kenyan.'

'But your mother was English?'

Hugo gave a curt nod. His mother had been dead a long time – that territory was off-limits.

'Then you are also ours, I'm afraid. You hold a

British passport.' The young man's eyes jumped nervously to the old woman at his side as if asking for more instructions.

'So, Hugo,' said the crone, fixing him with her steely gaze. 'Do you wish to spend the rest of your days in jail?'

Something in her tone prompted Hugo to look at her properly. When she had come in, he had swiftly discounted her because she was a woman – and an old one at that. He now took time to revise his opinion, noting the visual clues: silver-grey hair cut short; small but tough; unusual brooch in the shape of a serpent on her lapel; powerful and assured. Someone not to be dismissed.

'I don't fancy it much,' Hugo said with a shrug, trying to impress her with his cool. 'But I've been set up. It wasn't my fault.'

The woman tutted impatiently. 'Really, Hugo, you can't shirk all responsibility for what you did. You tried to kill a girl younger and weaker than yourself. Look at what you did for what it is.'

Hugo glared at her. He didn't like people holding up his actions for inspection. In his own mind, he was noble, a warrior; this woman had just described him as a coward.

'But at least you understand that you have no

future if you stay in this cell,' she continued. 'So I've come to make you an offer. Bernard, perhaps you'd like to go outside for a moment?'

It was presented as a request, but sounded more like an order.

'Are you sure?' Bernard asked, casting an anxious look at Hugo.

Hugo took satisfaction from the fact that the man was clearly afraid of him.

'Don't worry – I promise I won't harm him.' The woman gave Hugo a wintry smile.

'Yes, ma'am.'

Bernard backed out of the cell, leaving the two of them alone. The woman let the silence stretch for a moment, showing that she had no qualms being there with him.

'My name is Gladys Smith, Hugo. You have brought yourself to the attention of my employers and we were wondering if you would like to work for us – as an alternative, you understand, to spending the rest of your youth stewing in a concrete cell.'

'Put like that then I suppose I'm going to say "yes",' growled Hugo. 'Who are you exactly?'

'British Intelligence. We've had great success recently with a young operative and were thinking of expanding in that direction. You have been suggested as possible material for recruitment.'

'Me? Why?'

Gladys Smith paced the cell, pondering the question. 'You have certain . . . qualities that we feel have been misdirected by your upbringing. We want to retrain you – turn your skills in a more productive direction.'

Hugo thought about this, wondering what qualities he had demonstrated recently that would endear him to the spies.

'You want me to kill for you rather than for my father?' he asked bluntly.

The old woman actually laughed at that. 'Perhaps, but that wasn't what I had in mind. Espionage is more about blending in than blasting a way through. I should mention at this point that whatever your decision, I can give you no guarantees. We have a training facility in the southwest of England. If you choose to try it out but fail to stay the course, you'll find yourself back behind bars. If you make a run for it – well, let's say that might be the last thing you do.'

'Where can I run to?' Hugo asked bleakly. 'I've no money, no family any more. No friends.'

'Quite. So you understand the position?'

'Yeah, I'm up to my neck in this dung heap and you're offering me a different pile to shovel.'

'One without bars attached.' Gladys Smith paused, looking him over again. 'You might want to consider the possibility that you will enjoy it.'

Truro, England: Fresh breeze from the south, 18°C

Outside the front doors of Truro Secondary School, Darcie was conscious of being the only new pupil of her age as she waited alone for the bell to ring. The intake of eleven year olds were easy to spot as they were dressed in crisp-from-the-shop uniforms, clustered shyly in small groups of those who knew each other from primary school. The older pupils declared their familiarity with the whole routine by quickly colonising their favourite corners of the grounds and taking no notice of the newcomers.

Darcie just didn't know how to behave. All her previous experience had been in international schools scattered around the world. Though far apart, they had been essentially the same: privileged kids in small classes, high standards and firm discipline. Going on what she knew, she'd come in a neat uniform and tie done up in the conventional manner, thinking that was the best way to blend in. But now she saw that that was wrong – way out of step. She felt like she'd landed on an alien planet. Here the children had wrecked their uniform before even walking through the gates: ties off, shirts hanging out. There were masses of them – over a thousand, she guessed. She was lost.

A bell rang and the front doors opened. The teacher who had unlocked them stood to one side and nodded mournfully to the pupils flooding past her. The school year was grinding into motion again like a clapped-out old car about to fail its annual inspection.

'Excuse me, miss,' said Darcie. 'I'm new. Can you tell me where I should go?'

The teacher looked Darcie up and down with a professional eye. 'How old are you?'

'Fourteen.'

'Right, go and talk to reception.' She waved vaguely over her shoulder. 'Don't get swept up with the new intake or you'll end up in Year Seven.'

Thanking her, Darcie walked over to the reception desk.

'Hi, I'm –'

'Darcie Galt?' A brisk-mannered secretary with her glasses on a chain around her neck smiled at her. 'I recognize you from your file. Welcome to Truro. You're in Mr Murray's form. You need to be in registration, room six, red corridor.'

'Where's –?'

'Here's a map.' The secretary passed her a clear plastic folder with a map on the front. 'All the other information you'll need about the school is in there. All right, dear?'

'Er, yes, I suppose.'

Wandering with map in hand, Darcie managed to find the right room on the second attempt. Knocking once, she entered, interrupting the teacher in mid flow as he made his way down the register. Thirty pairs of eyes locked on her. She had the sudden image of herself as a rabbit caught in headlights.

'Darcie, is it?' said the teacher, a small man with thick dark hair wearing a suit that looked like a survivor from the 1970s, wide lapels and flared trousers.

'Yes, sir.'

'Class, this is Darcie Galt, the new girl I told you about. Come from . . . where was it you come from exactly?'

'Brussels,' Darcie said quickly. Not strictly true –

she had last lived in Belgium when she was six, but she hoped it sounded too boring to invite more penetrating follow-up questions.

'That was it. Now, Kayleigh and Chantelle, you have just volunteered to show our new class member around.' Two blonde girls in the front row smiled half- heartedly at her and returned their attention to their bubblegum-pink nails. 'Take a seat, Darcie, while I finish taking the register.'

Choosing a chair near her guides, Darcie glanced around the room. The attention she was attracting wasn't exactly hostile, but neither did it seem very welcoming. She guessed that they had already settled into a pattern in the class and someone late on the scene was like a meal that was hard to digest – a boa constrictor swallowing a goat. The odd thought made her smile. Her expression attracted the gaze of a fit-looking black boy, sitting by the window. He raised an eyebrow, asking her to share the joke. She shook her head slightly but kept on grinning.

She couldn't blame them for looking her over, wondering how she'd slot in. That wouldn't be with Kayleigh and Chantelle, Darcie could tell that already. At a guess, they were the princess of fashion type – manicured, lots of make-up, seriously into clothes. Sport was more Darcie's thing – football and fencing to be precise. In a school this size there was bound to be a soccer team she could join. The sooner she found cover among a group of girls like herself, the better. Having spent the last five months attracting a very dangerous sort of attention, she wanted nothing more than to disappear into the crowd for a bit.

'Hey, Darcie, wasn't it?'

Darcie looked up and saw that the class was on their feet, Chantelle standing in front of her.

'Yeah, that's right.'

'Cool. Let's go.'

'What's first?'

'Physics. Can you believe it: first day, first period, and we get physics?'

Darcie grimaced in sympathy, although she was actually looking forward to getting back in to the normality of lessons.

The class was hanging around outside the lab waiting for the teacher to open the door. Chantelle and Kayleigh drifted off to chat with some other girls. Darcie leaned against the wall, trying to look as if she didn't mind standing on her own. Her guides didn't appear very enthusiastic about making her feel welcome.

'Hey, new girl, nice tie,' mocked the boy she had

noticed earlier. He was waiting a few paces away. Closer to, she saw that his hair was shaved in a pattern of swirls; a string of wooden beads at his throat was not quite hidden by his school shirt. Good-looking – and apparently well aware of the fact – he leaned against the wall, surrounded by a huddle of hangers-on. But he had something about him – a sense of fun and liveliness – that made him stand out from the crowd.

'Thanks.' Darcie played her answer straight.

'So, what're you into?' he asked, folding his arms and moving to lounge against the wall beside her. He was taller than her but she rather liked that as she often found herself towering over boys her age.

'What d'you mean?'

'Music 'n' stuff.'

'Oh.' She reeled off a list of her favourite bands, throwing in a few west African ones she listened to in Kenya. She was sure no one here would have heard of them.

'Seriously? You like Youssou N'dour?' the boy asked, pushing himself off the wall. He dropped his 'too cool for you' act and seemed genuinely interested.

'Yeah.' She wondered if it had been the wrong thing to say.

'Brutal. He's the Man, sister.' He held out his hand in a low five. 'I'm Jake. What's your name again?'

'Darcie.' She brushed her hand across his.

'Well, Darcie, welcome to the back of beyond.' He glanced over at Kayleigh and Chantelle. 'When the Sugababes have finished showing you around, come find me.'

A boy next to Jake sniggered and received an elbow in the stomach in payment.

'Sure. I'll do that.' Darcie gave him a smile.

'Yeah, see that you do.'

Darcie sailed through lessons that morning. Though she'd missed quite a lot of school before the summer break thanks to the injuries sustained in Nairobi, she found she was well ahead on most subjects. The physics teacher's eyes brightened when he found a girl who was not chewing her split ends or staring out the window.

French was a waste of time for her as she was fluent and most of her classmates were still struggling with buying baguettes. The teacher, Mrs Newman, got her involved in role-playing conversations in front of the class with Jake, but Darcie was reluctant to be picked out. She didn't want the reputation of teacher's pet. She needn't have worried because Jake's exuberant but wildly inaccurate French had everyone in stitches.

'Jake, you have the accent, the mannerisms and the soul of the language; all you need now is the grammar,' announced Mrs Newman, wiping tears of laughter from her eyes as she dismissed the class. 'But Darcie, I think you might be better off learning a different language or you'll be bored to death. We offer Italian, German and Spanish. Tell me what you want to do and I'll see if I can juggle your timetable.'

Darcie didn't feel it was a good time to mention that she already had a grounding in all those languages so just nodded.

Chantelle and Kayleigh had gone by the time Mrs Newman let her go. Darcie made her way out into the sunshine on her own. The girls were nowhere to be seen. In fact, there were very few outside at all, only boys who had commandeered the playground for football.

Football.

Though it was a risk to attract attention to herself on her first day, particularly when no other girls were playing, Darcie couldn't help herself: her feet were already running. She could see Jake in midfield. Well, he'd said to come and find him. Slipping on her trainers, she dumped her bag with the boys' stuff and ran on to the pitch.

'Whoa!' shouted a sixth-former in goal when he spotted the invasion. He held his arms out to stop her. 'Netball's the other way.'

Darcie dodged past him. 'Don't play netball.'

Jake had the ball and was making good progress up the field towards goal. His team had their ties around their heads. As hers was still round her neck, that made her the opposition. Darcie darted forward, stole the ball from him with a hoot of laughter and shot up the centre. Foiling two attempts to tackle her, she shot at goal – and scored. The goalie looked disgusted with himself.

'Not fair!' shouted Jake, holding his arms out in protest. 'I didn't know she was playing.'

'Way to go, new girl!' shouted the sixth-former, who had rapidly changed his mind about blocking her. 'You can be on my team any day.'

Darcie's new teammates grinned at her. The ball went into play again and the game got more competitive. The head-ties wanted revenge: every time the ball went near Darcie they would descend on her in force – but she was good, having been up against such tactics a lot from the boys at her last school. The desire to beat her was tipping some over into cheating. One ginger-haired lad pulled on her shirt to hold her back from the ball, swinging her round so she hit the deck. Jake ran over and punched him in the arm.

'Hey, cut it out!' Jake warned.

The boy looked sheepish and mumbled an apology. He extended a hand to Darcie to help her up.

'That's a penalty at least,' said the sixth-former. Jake nodded. 'Yeah. You take a crack at it, Darcie.'

She could feel them all watching her as she lined up the ball. A bell rang for the end of break, but none of them were leaving until they knew if she could beat the goalie again. She didn't feel nervous – she felt great. Taking a short run, she struck the ball sweetly and it sailed in over the goalie's outstretched fingers. Immediately, she was hoisted from behind by her teammates.

'Two–nil!' they cheered.

The big sixth-former jogged over, waving his shirt away from his body where he'd got overheated.

'That was great. You really can play. I'm Max by the way. What's your name?'

'Darcie Galt.'

His eyes widened. 'Are you related to Ken Galt by any chance?'

He must mean Stingo. 'Yeah, he's my . . . my

cousin. I'm staying with his parents.' She hoped the cover story would hold up.

'Ken Galt's cousin – fantastic! He's a bit of a legend around here, as you'll find out if you stick around Truro for long.'

Jake reappeared at her side with her bag. 'Next time, you're on my team, twinkletoes.'

'Or maybe I'll let you on mine, if I pick you,' she teased.

'Yeah, maybe.' He laughed. 'I'd better put some practice in or you'll leave me on the subs bench. Come on, then: geography next. I'll show you where to go.'

[3]

Westminster, London: Sunny, clouding over later, 20°C

Christopher Lock, Director of Regional Affairs at Secret Intelligence Services, waited outside the foreign secretary's office in King Charles Street feeling immensely pleased with himself. The over-lush Victorian décor, recently restored with its frescoes, gold leaf and red velvet drapes, reflected back his self-esteem – empire and authority: just right for the reinvigorated Christopher Lock. Only a few months ago, as he approached retirement, he had picked up mutterings that his colleagues had written him off, circling his position like sharks surrounding a wounded diver. But he had proved them wrong – stamped his authority on his department and astonished his superiors (and there weren't many of those these days) with his handling of the Kenyan and Egyptian situations. He had taken risks which, if events had gone differently, could have seen him end his days ignominiously; but, thanks to his granddaughter, the gamble had paid off.

The willingness to dare was the mark of a great man, thought Christopher, giving himself a mental pat on the back.

As his sixty-fifth birthday loomed, there were already rumours that he would be asked to stay on to oversee the new initiative to recruit young agents. The prime minister had put his foot down over involving anyone under sixteen again – Darcie Lock had proved a huge success but the prime minister felt that she was an exceptional case and a political liability – but youngsters of military age were thought to be fair game. The only problem was that there was no budget. The first new recruit – a boy Christopher personally identified as being perfect material for such an assignment – had begun training in a very hand-to-mouth fashion – not ideal at all. Considering the sensitivity of the initiative, it was hardly something for which you could go to the Treasury with begging bowl in hand. No, it would have to be squeezed out of someone, somehow – and Christopher Lock had an instinct that the foreign secretary was the one to approach.

The private secretary, right-hand man to the minister, came out into the waiting room. Despite his neat suit, he looked as if he'd missed a few appointments with his barber, auburn hair long enough to brush his collar and bags under his brown eyes.

'Mr Lock, the minister is ready for you now.'

'Thank you, James. How's the new baby?' Christopher was not particularly interested in the answer but always made a point of being briefed on the personal lives of those with influence.

James Harlem dropped his professional manner for a moment and grinned. 'Mother and child doing well, sir.' To Christopher's relief, James resisted the urge to get out the inevitable photo in his wallet.

'You really should take more advantage of parental leave,' said Christopher, wagging a friendly finger at the new father. He, of course, had never taken a day off in his life for his own son and didn't believe in such new-fangled ideas, but he calculated that the foreign secretary could hear him and it was the kind of thing that would go down well with this breed of politician.

'Ah, Christopher! How are you?' The grey-haired man with smoker's yellow teeth got up from behind his desk and came around to shake hands. He steered his visitor to the sofa, while he took an armchair and James perched on an upright seat. The minister fidgeted with excess energy; the plush surroundings were clearly unable to soothe and contain a man more used to standing on picket lines than pushing paper across a leather-topped desk.

He's looking old, thought Christopher, studying the foreign secretary as they exchanged a few words of small talk. He remembered the file he had once seen on John Riddell. It started when the minister had been a student radical. MI5 had kept an eye on him during the feverish days of the late seventies and had taken many amusing photos of this pillar of society lounging around at protests with shaggy hair and an equally shaggy Afghan coat. Ridiculous though he looked, he had also glowed with youth and vitality.

Now John Riddell is old and soured like the rest of us, Christopher mused, finding great satisfaction in the thought. The free spirit trapped in the responsibilities of an adult. Travelled from left to right of the political spectrum like so many do.

'Thank you for coming in this morning – and for your latest briefing – all very informative.' Riddell handed the papers to James Harlem and sat back, unaware he was tapping out a Bob Dylan song with his fingers. 'I have a last-minute request to make of you and your people, Christopher.'

Lock smiled. This was fortunate. If he did Riddell a favour, it would make the money matter much easier.

'I would be delighted to be of assistance, sir.'

'Good, good.' Riddell relaxed, hugging his ankle, knee lolling sideways.

When had politics become so informal? wondered Christopher. Meetings were more like daytime TV chat shows than affairs of state. He missed the old days before first names, sofas and political correctness.

'I've been asked by the UN secretary general if we can co-host peace talks between the Russians and the Tazbeks. As you probably know, she is acting as mediator.'

Christopher nodded curtly. Of course, he knew all about Secretary General Lopez's attempt to end the punishing civil war between Russia and its oil-rich breakaway province of Tazbekistan. He personally thought it highly unlikely she would succeed as Russia was not going to allow such a jewel in its crown to slip away, whatever the human cost, and the Tazbeks showed no sign of settling for anything short of independence.

'Why does she want to come to the UK, sir?'

'The Americans are refusing visas to the Tazbek delegation. The CIA claim they're terrorists, which of course they are: that's rather the point of holding the negotiations in the first place.'

'So she can't hold talks in New York?'

'Exactly. The Russians and the Tazbeks have agreed that Britain is a neutral player in this particular dispute, so they are willing to come here. Relations with the Russians have been so difficult lately, it suits us to be seen to do them a favour.'

'When do the delegates arrive, minister?'

'Next Thursday – that's the problem. It gives us very little time to find a secure venue and make the necessary arrangements. We need somewhere out of the public eye. Ms Lopez wants to lock them away until they agree. Gleneagles can't take us at such short notice as they've got some big golf shenanigans going on, so we're running out of ideas.'

'Isn't this more a matter for MI5 and the diplomatic protection squad?'

Riddell dropped his ankle and leaned forward. 'Of course, but I want to borrow something of yours for the week.'

Christopher raised an eyebrow, waiting.

'St Helen's.'

The director of special operations nodded. That made perfect sense: his department's training centre down in the West Country would be ideal. Almost an island, it was easy to defend. Exceedingly well equipped, it could accommodate guests to the highest standard and the staff were used to hosting conferences. The only niggle was having to hand the place over to their sister operation, MI5, for the duration. His own people wouldn't like the thought of them crawling all over St Helen's, but then he could hardly refuse on those grounds.

'Of course, sir. We are delighted to be of help. I'll make the necessary arrangements.'

Riddell nodded his thanks, already flicking through his briefing papers to his next meeting. 'And, of course, I'd like the latest intelligence you have on the Tazbek situation. I want us to assist the secretary general in every way we can.'

Christopher could not help smiling to himself.

The foreign secretary and the secretary general were known to have a warm friendship since spending a tour of African countries in each other's company. It had been the source of many gentle jokes in the House of Commons and in the press. The story was helped along by the fact that Carmen Lopez was the youngest and by far the most glamorous Secretary General the UN had ever seen. She was also ambitious, breathing new life into an organisation that had seemed to lose its way.

'Of course, sir. In fairness to my colleagues, I must point out that the change will entail some extra expenditure in our training budget as we'll have to reschedule a whole raft of courses and relocate agents. Can I take it that you have a budget to cover this?'

Riddell frowned and looked to his private secretary.

'We do have a special emergency fund – I'm sure we can wangle something. I'll get our finance people to talk to yours,' said James.

'Excellent. That seems to be that.' The foreign secretary stood up. 'I must make tracks. The Chinese trade minister is in town. Lunch.'

'He likes chess and gardening,' Christopher said automatically as he too rose to his feet.

'Really? You are a useful man to know, Christopher.' Riddell rubbed his hands together. 'I can never think of anything to say to these chaps in between courses but now I'll be fine. How is your granddaughter, by the way?'

Only the very senior members of the cabinet knew about Darcie's recent exploits.

'Disappeared, sir.'

The two men exchanged knowing looks. 'Good. You wouldn't believe how the Americans are still bending my ear about her. President Morris is mortally afraid someone will dig her up the day before election night and blow his campaign out of the water.' They walked to the door and Riddell laid a hand on Christopher's arm to hold him back a second. 'They've started legal proceedings, you know?'

'Proceedings?' Christopher was pulled up short: here was something he didn't know and he didn't like it.

'Custody – allegedly on behalf of the mother but my sources say they've sent her off for retraining in Alaska and I bet she knows nothing about it.'

'But if they can't prove Darcie's here . . .'

'Exactly. Try and keep it that way because if they get her on their soil we won't be able to do anything to help. She's political dynamite so you'd probably not see your granddaughter again for some time.'

Christopher didn't need the warning; he understood the position very well. 'Of course, sir. Enjoy your lunch.'

A very useful meeting, Christopher reflected as he returned to his car in the courtyard. Extra money obtained without needing to describe exactly what for; the foreign secretary in his debt; and a heads-up on Darcie. Extremely satisfactory.

St Helen's, Cornwall: Sunny spells, 18°C

Hugo Kraus looked down the sights of his rifle and squeezed the trigger. The recoil of the gun pushed hard against his shoulder as he let out controlled sprays of bullets, all finding their mark in the centre of his target. It was the kind of task for which he felt he was made: something he could master, something that needed a cool head and steady hands. He reloaded his semi-automatic machine gun with a new clip of ammunition and took careful aim.

Hugo was enjoying one of his rare moments of

peace; he had found that by fixing all his attention on the bull's eye he could silence the voices in his head. They had plagued him in his cell, driving him into bouts of silent fury; now these fits were less common – non-existent when he had a gun in hand and a target on which to concentrate. He had come to think of these voices as his enemies – invaders that threatened to allow emotion to sweep back over the barrenness inside him. It was better for him if they were ignored as he knew he couldn't handle what they said. He wasn't listening.

'Excellent, Kraus,' said Commander Barratt, standing behind his pupil who lay outstretched on the floor of the rifle range, 'very good. Not much to teach you here, is there?'

Hugo sprang to his feet, pleased with his performance. Commander Barratt was notoriously hard to please; a few words of praise from him were worth whole speeches from others. 'Thank you, sir.'

'Report to me at twenty hundred hours for your SNE. For now: dismissed!'

SIS's newest recruit checked his rifle back in at the armoury and jogged back to his room. Eight o'clock: that gave him three hours of spare time before his solo nighttime expedition. The time couldn't pass quickly enough for Hugo: he loved the role play these outings allowed – the camouflage paint and crawling around in the Cornish sand dunes to 'win' some objective from the 'enemy'. He liked it best when he was up against another player. He'd absolutely destroyed that man last week – and he, an agent of two years' experience! Hugo had stolen his mission brief from right under his nose by lighting a diversionary campfire. It was basic psychology: people assume light means people. It draws their eyes. Look behind you, Hugo had wanted to whisper as he crawled away with the palmtop in his pocket.

Hugo walked under the archway of St Helen's House. Formerly a medieval castle, the knights had long since gone from its chambers, replaced now by civil servants of a very select kind. With thick stone walls, built to withstand the sea winds and hostile invaders, it had the feeling of a fortress on the outside, but inside it had been renovated to the standards of a superior hotel. This wasn't for the benefit of the trainees but for the private conferences of senior government figures that occasionally descended upon the college. Hugo wasn't complaining; anything was better than a Kenyan cell and even his little room in the attic had its own bathroom and superb view across to the mainland.

Gladys Smith had been right – he was enjoying

himself, finding an outlet for his anger and aggression in the physical and weapons training that formed a large part of his day. He thought he might have even reached the point where he could hear the name 'Darcie Lock' and not immediately want to break something.

Gladys Smith was waiting for her student in the hall, sitting beneath a portrait of Sir Raoul Tregethick as she read through some papers. As his most trusted friend and colleague, Christopher Lock had asked her to take up the position as head of the trial training scheme for young agents while she waited for her next posting abroad. She'd been happy to oblige, though she had to admit that a seventeen-year-old killer was the last souvenir she imagined she would be bringing back with her from Nairobi.

'Good day, Hugo?' she asked briskly as she got to her feet.

'Yes, ma'am.' Hugo had treated his boss with genuine respect ever since she had managed to floor him in their first self-defence class a month ago.

'I'm afraid there's going to be a change of plan for the next few weeks,' she continued, guiding him towards her office overlooking the main gate. 'The other students are being diverted to Sunningdale so there will be no cryptology course next week.'

Hugo tried to look disappointed but the time spent in the classroom was not his favourite part of the day. 'So what's happening to me?'

'In view of the fact that you are still on probation, we thought it best to keep you here under our surveillance.'

Hugo nodded. He expected as much. They still thought he might make a run for it, so he was under strict curfew and tagged at all times.

'Actually, I've decided you can learn a lot more about security by seeing it in operation. There's a peace conference coming here – a very big deal – big names. The boys in blue will be with us from tonight and you've been allocated a role as their runner.'

'Their what?'

'General dogsbody, tea boy.'

Hugo frowned but dared not protest – not to her.

'And while you are asking how many sugars they take, you can shadow them and find out what they do. I've straightened it out with the police – you'll work with the diplomatic protection squad.'

That sounded more like it. 'I'm sure I'll learn a lot, ma'am.'

'I know you will. Meanwhile, I'm off for a few days myself to see if I can find you some suitable classmates. No point having a training scheme for a glorious total of one, is there?'

Hugo wondered what kind of recruits she was thinking of – it would be good to have some other young people around. 'Where are you looking?'

'I'm turning the stones over to see what crawls out,' she said enigmatically, waving him out of the door. 'Like I did with you.'

Truro, England: Rain from the west expected later, 17°C

Darcie still got a thrill to see Jake waiting for her at the school gate as he had every day since they had started seeing each other. They weren't officially 'going out' but the school rumour mill seemed to think it was only a matter of time. Today Jake was leaning against the concrete post, chatting to Max Gerrans. Both boys turned to greet her when she approached.

'Hey, Darcie, any news from Ken Galt?' Max leapt in with his question. As a keen member of the local Cadet Corps, Max had told her about all the records Stingo set when he belonged – most of them were still unbroken. He had been angling for an introduction for weeks now.

'Sorry, no,' said Darcie. 'I'll let you know if I hear when he's next down. Though I should warn you – he usually drops in unexpectedly and is off again immediately.'

Max nodded as if it was no more than he would expect from his hero. 'You've got my number if he does. I want to ask him about the army.'

'Thinking of joining up?' asked Jake, laughing. 'Yeah, I can see you with a buzz cut and camouflage gear.'

Max didn't crack a smile. 'So can I. See you later.'

Darcie followed Jake to the form room, thinking how strange it was that, in only a month, somewhere that had been so foreign now seemed like home. And it was all thanks to Jake. She had to admit that she spent a lot of time when she wasn't with him, thinking about him.

'Did you do the maths homework?' Jake asked.

'Yeah, did it last night.' Marcus and Claire were very conscientious about their guardian duties and made sure she did all her work the moment she got home from school.

'Can I copy?'

'OK. What were you up to yesterday?' She handed her file over.

'Dad's got a catering job at St Helen's this week – needed some help setting up.' He began mechanically writing down her work until he spotted a mistake. 'I'd better not give the same wrong answer – bit of a give-away.' He grinned at her as he wrote down the right solution.

Darcie rolled her eyes. 'Pinch my work and go and get better marks than me.' She pulled her book from him and corrected her own mistake. 'I don't think so.'

'You're very competitive, d'you know that, Darcie?' Jake tugged the book back.

'And you're not?'

'Course I am – but I'm male: I'm pre-programmed to want to thump all the other cavemen into submission.' He beat his chest, mock-Tarzan.

But Darcie didn't laugh; she felt a shiver up her spine. 'Don't talk like that, Jake. It creeps me out. You remind me of someone from my last school – a boy called Hugo Kraus.'

'You know I was only joking.' Jake put his file away and handed hers back. 'Boyfriend, was he?'

'Definitely not. He was a nightmare – no, really, don't laugh. He wasn't the least bit funny.'

'What he do? Snap the head off your Barbie?' They headed for history together.

'Do I look like the kind of girl that would've had Barbies?'

'Yeah – and I bet you liked pink.'

'Take that back, Jake Bridges!'

'Or what? What'yer goin' to do, Darcie-babe?'

'I'll tell everyone you wear Thomas the Tank Engine pyjamas.'

'Argh, no! My secret's out! How did you find out?' He grabbed the textbook she was carrying and raced off. She chased him down the corridor, wrestled the book from him and hit him over the head to the cheers of the rest of the class.

'All right, all right! I surrender!' he laughed.

The history corridor was on the ground floor, not far from the entrance hall. The Darcie-and-Jake sideshow over, the class piled into the room as soon as Miss Jones allowed them in to invade her space. She had been the teacher who had met Darcie on the door on the first day; a month on and she looked exhausted by the term that had only just got fully underway. Her lessons also felt a bit tired, limping from event to event. Most of the class passed the time they should have spent learning about the Middle East doodling in their books. Darcie knew she should be interested considering her own recent history in that region, but somehow the information kept sliding through her brain like a train that wasn't stopping at the station.

She gazed out the window idly as a police car parked by the headmaster's Volvo and three men got out. Probably the drugs awareness team – there was a talk on that theme this afternoon. The policemen disappeared through the front entrance. A black sports car drew up; a single passenger got out. Darcie scribbled some more notes. Only another hour to go and then it would be mid-morning break and a chance for more football. Her turn to pick the team and she was still trying to decide if she was going to choose Jake first or not. Sometimes it was more fun to play against him.

Deep into the collective slumber, the door to the classroom opened abruptly. Darcie sat up with a jolt, transfixed by the person standing on the threshold: it was Gladys Smith, her old mentor from Nairobi. Even before the intelligence agent said anything, Darcie began packing her bag, suddenly wide-awake. If Agent Smith were here, that must mean . . .

'Sorry to interrupt, but I've come for Darcie,' Gladys said coolly, beckoning her old student.

Unsure what to do at this unexpected interruption, Miss Jones stared at the intruder. 'And you are?'

'A friend of the family.'

Darcie was already on her feet, moving to the front of the room.

'Darcie, where're you going?' called Jake.

Please, no, not again. 'Dentist,' she said, hating the lie. 'I forgot – have to hurry.'

Gladys took Darcie's arm and guided her into the corridor. American voices could be heard coming their way, apparently in loud discussion with the head-teacher. Gladys swung smartly on her heel and marched straight back into the classroom.

'Excuse me.' She elbowed Kayleigh aside and threw the window open. 'After you, Darcie.'

With an agonised look at Jake, Darcie leapt out the window, landing painfully in the roses of the school's millennium garden. Gladys vaulted after her, avoiding the thorns, and strode purposefully towards the black sports car parked in the caretaker's spot. Darcie could feel the stares of her classmates on her back like a sunlamp. What must they be thinking?

'Quick as you can,' said Agent Smith, unlocking the car at ten metres.

Darcie dived into the passenger seat as Gladys

started the engine. From leaving her seat to driving out of school, less than sixty seconds had elapsed.

'I hope I didn't interrupt anything interesting?' asked Gladys as the car wound its way through the backstreets of Truro.

'Not really. Nice to see you too, Mrs Smith.' Darcie scrunched her knees up to her chest as what had just happened began to sink in.

'Yes, sorry about that, there wasn't time. I'm pleased to see you again – I certainly wasn't expecting it so soon.'

'So why have you come? What's this all about?'

'Ah. *This* is the American consular officer coming to take you into his custody on behalf of your mother. Your grandfather found out just in time. Sent the call through only half an hour ago – hence the unexpected interruption to your lesson.'

'How did you get here so fast?'

'Not from Nairobi, obviously. I'm staying just down the road. That's where I'm taking you now – it's less than ideal but we don't have any choice now the Americans have taken off the gloves.'

The car turned on to the road to the south coast.

Darcie was seething: yet another uprooting – yanked away from her mates without so much as a by your leave. She hadn't even had a chance to say goodbye to Jake before heading out for what she suspected was about to be the longest dental appointment in history.

'How did the Americans know where I was?'

'Warrant Officer Galt.'

'Stingo wouldn't tell them!'

'Obviously not. But they've been doing their homework. Galt is not a very common name and they discovered an Officer Corps bulletin board where a military man seemed to be the main topic of discussion, particularly since his cousin had turned up at the local school.'

'Oh.' Thanks, Max Gerrans and his hero-complex.

'Not hard to follow the trail after that.' Reaching a copse, Gladys turned the car on to a track winding through the trees towards a perimeter fence. Flashing her badge at the security gates, they hummed into motion and she drove through.

'Why can't the Americans just leave me alone?' Darcie asked plaintively. In this mood she hardly had eyes for the beautiful scenery that now surrounded her: cliffs, beaches far below, a thin ribbon of road leading to what looked like a fairytale castle on a headland.

'Why indeed. Perhaps, then, it has nothing to do

with the fact that you could torpedo their man's chance of being re-elected?'

'Still, why would I want to tell anybody anything? I just want to get back to a normal life.'

'They don't trust you to do that – nor would I in their shoes.' Gladys slowed for a cattle grid.

'So why are you taking the risk of annoying them?'

'Because you're one of ours, Darcie, and SIS doesn't give any of us up without a fight.'

Gladys pulled the car up by the stable block round the back of St Helen's. She turned off the ignition and sat for a moment tapping the steering wheel – a rare sign of uncertainty from her. 'I've brought you here because the Americans will be unable to follow us – it's a training college belonging to my department, very well guarded, off limits. But there's something I should mention before you get out of the car.'

'What's that?'

'There's someone here that I'd rather you didn't meet.'

'Fine – just tell me what he looks like and I'll keep my distance.'

Gladys shook her head. 'It's not as easy as that:

you both know each other and you won't be able to avoid crossing paths.'

Darcie couldn't think whom she meant. 'We do? Who is it?'

'Hugo Kraus.'

'No! You have to be joking.' Darcie felt a sudden urge, whether to cry or laugh – or both – she couldn't decide. It was bad enough losing her new life without Gladys making ill-timed jests about her past.

'I'm utterly serious. It is unfortunate that this has happened so soon, but he's here – that's a fact – and you're both going to have to deal with it.'

[4]

MI6 Headquarters, Vauxhall, London: Changeable, 20°C

Michael Lock sipped the whisky his father had poured him as he admired the view of the Thames through the window. The water rolled by, gunmetal grey under a cloudy sky – one of those nondescript days that London excelled in. A day of umbrellas held ready but not deployed; coats shrugged on and off as rain threatened. The weather was holding the city prisoner. Just as he felt trapped in this period of not knowing; of powerlessness.

'So you managed to pull her out just in time?' Michael addressed his father's back.

Christopher turned around from the drinks tray, glass in hand, and smiled – his mouth in a tight line. 'That's right. Gladys was in the area already so there was nothing to worry about.'

'But you still didn't see fit to tell me. My daughter was about to be extradited – or whatever the word is for children – and you forgot to mention it to me.' Michael's tone was hopeless: he knew his father better than to expect full disclosure or even trust. As both son and employee, he had no chance of being treated as an equal.

Christopher took a seat behind his desk and swirled his whisky, clinking the ice against the glass. 'The Yanks were doing it in Ginnie's name. Hasn't your wife mentioned it?'

'Father, you and I both know that she had nothing to do with the action!'

'Clever though, on their part. Quite a plausible story too: young girl meets suspect army guy on the internet and ends up shacked up with his eccentric parents – no wonder they had the courts here bending over backwards to help. I'm surprised it hasn't leaked to the tabloids. You, I'm afraid, were portrayed as the absent and uncaring father.'

'That's obscene.' Michael was angry but not

surprised: nothing President Morris did to silence Darcie would shock him now.

'Yes, yes, of course it is. Can we move on, Michael? I've a lot to get through. What do you propose we do with Darcie?'

Michael put his glass down with a thump. 'You're asking me?'

'Of course. You are her father, aren't you?'

'You never bothered to ask my opinion before.'

'Do you want to turn this into an argument about the past or shall we deal with the rather more urgent present?'

Michael gave a curt nod. 'So she's at St Helen's.'

'Yes.'

'With Gladys?'

'Yes. And half the diplomatic protection squad as the peace conference is about to roll in.' He decided not to mention Hugo Kraus's presence – Michael was bound not to understand. He was a little touchy on the subject of Kraus since he'd seen him trying to kill Darcie.

'What about her education?'

'We could arrange for a tutor.'

'But she can't stay in limbo forever.'

'I think none of this will be necessary beyond November. Once the votes are cast, no one in the

White House will be interested in what becomes of her. She can return to normal life – of a sort.'

Michael was quick to pounce. 'You're not to use her again, Father. Do you understand?'

Christopher smiled serenely. 'Don't you think I've learned my lesson, Michael?'

Michael Lock gave a sceptical grunt. 'All right. She sounds safe enough for the moment. Can I contact her?'

'Of course, though I suggest you use a secure channel as we don't want the Americans listening in. You have Gladys's number, I suppose?'

'Yes. And what can we do for Warrant Officer Galt?'

'Who?' Christopher frowned.

'The SAS man. Sounds like he's been saddled with a nasty rumour about his relationship to Darcie – he doesn't deserve that. He's been our staunch ally throughout.'

'Not sure there's a lot we can do.' Christopher stared into the air over his son's head, fingertips touching. 'He'll live it down.'

'The least I can do is talk to his parents, put their minds at rest that nothing inappropriate has gone on.'

Christopher marvelled that after all these years

his son was still such an idealist, trying to put everything to rights. He was sure he had been much younger than Michael when he learned that the world was broken beyond fixing. 'Yes, do that if you think it will help. And then what?'

'And then I suppose I'd better think about my future – where Ginnie and I should go.'

'How long are they keeping her in Alaska?'

'Six weeks.'

'Until after the elections?'

'Yes. No coincidence that.'

'No, it wouldn't be. Well then, I suggest you take this opportunity to refresh your own skills – there are a number of courses I think you could benefit from. After that, I'll have something to put to you.'

St Helen's, Cornwall: Unsettled weather, spots of rain, 16°C

Darcie hid in her bedroom for the rest of the day, her whole body shaking with a poisonous mixture of anger and fear. It was not fair to expect her to live under the same roof as the boy who had tried to kill her. Not right. He should be locked up – not let out and trained to be even more dangerous. Gladys said he had changed – was still changing. She had described him as a victim of his upbringing.

'He's been brutalised by that father of his,' Gladys had argued as they sat in the car. 'We won't be able to turn back the clock but surely it is far better for someone like that to be working on our side than against?'

Darcie emphatically did not agree. It would be far better if Hugo were not able to work for anyone. And as for 'sides', Gladys may know what she meant by that, but Darcie was very confused as to where her own loyalty lay. With her family and friends for sure, but country? What country? If she was uncertain, that must mean Hugo, dragged out of a prison in Kenya, was more so.

Darcie's first reaction had been to refuse to get out of the car. She stared straight through the windscreen, arms folded across her chest, in a kind of mental lockdown.

'Mrs Smith, please turn around and take me out of here.'

'No,' Gladys said flatly. 'If you want to walk out straight into the arms of the Americans then that is your affair. I'm not helping you. It is about a mile down the drive that way if you wish to leave.'

Darcie gazed at the line of trees that marked the edge of the estate, beyond which waited . . . waited what? 'I don't know what President Morris's people would do with me, but surely it can't be worse than Hugo Kraus.'

Mrs Smith took the keys out of the ignition.

'My guess is they will hide you away somewhere and refuse you any contact with anyone. Perhaps after a time they will forget where they put you. Do you want to risk finding out?'

Feeling trapped, Darcie mutely shook her head and climbed out of the car.

At least her room felt safe. Up in the top of the building, the window looked out to sea. The Cornish water sparkled blue in the intermittent sunshine – not the warm, rich turquoise of the Indian Ocean she was used to, but a cold, northern azure. Shadows of clouds chased across the surface, seeming as restless as she felt. It was late in the season to swim, but she wondered what it would be like to dive off the cliffs and into the water. She felt a longing to walk the pale sand of the beach and explore the caves. But that meant daring to go outside.

Come on, Darcie, she chided when she caught sight of her pale-faced reflection in the window. I know they've let him out but you mustn't allow that to make you a prisoner.

Besides, she wanted to find the kitchens. Jake had mentioned something about his father having a catering contract at St Helen's – it hadn't escaped her attention that she might get to say goodbye after all.

Taking a deep breath, she opened her door a crack. Silence. Running along the corridor, she took the stairs, two at a time, and darted through the entrance hall. A party of men laying cable looked up briefly then ignored her.

No Hugo.

Taking a left, she headed for the kitchen, beginning to feel more secure. The Hugo she remembered would not be anywhere near the servants' quarters. She dipped into the kitchen and saw four cooks slicing vegetables, chatting happily while a radio played West African music in the background. A chef with a gold stud in his ear looked up.

'Sorry, love, but you can't come in here – health and safety.'

Darcie hovered by the door. 'Are you Jake's dad by any chance?'

The man put his knife down and wiped his hands. 'Might be. What's he done now?'

She gave a relieved grin. 'Nothing. Can you tell him that Darcie says "hi" and sorry she had to bale out so quickly this morning?'

'So you're Darcie?'

She nodded.

'Pleased to meet you. I'm Kito – or Mr Bridges to you, I suppose, if you're after my son.' Kito roared with laughter at her wary expression.

'Don't you listen to him,' said a large black lady with a matronly bosom as she threw some carrots into a steamer. 'Kito Bridges, don't go scaring the girl.'

'All right, Josephine, I was just having some fun. I know all about this little lady – Jake hasn't stopped talking about her since she scored two goals against his team on her first day.'

Darcie flushed, feeling absurdly happy that Jake had mentioned her at home.

Kito winked. 'I'll pass him your message.'

'Oh, and can you tell him not to tell anyone else where I am?' Darcie added, realising she wasn't doing a very good job of keeping her whereabouts a mystery.

'You want that kept secret?'

She nodded.

'Is it the kind of secret where I tell someone to

make sure they tell no more than one other person? That's a leaky sort of secret.' He waved the colander at her.

She smiled sheepishly. 'Just tell him – no one else.'

'OK, Darcie, consider it done.'

Darcie walked back down the corridor feeling much happier. It had felt so wrong to run out on Jake; now there was even a chance he might be able to visit her. She wouldn't tell Mrs Smith – she was bound not to approve, but it was too late to do anything about it. All that was left now was to straighten things out with Marcus and Claire, send someone to fetch her stuff and . . .

A tall boy with short blond hair was walking down the corridor towards her; he had a strong profile, square jaw and cold blue eyes. For the moment, he was looking at his fingers and muttering, 'Two with sugar, five without; two with sugar, five without.' Darcie stopped dead in her tracks, moving to put her back against the wall. Her knees shook; she wanted to be sick. Then the boy caught sight of her and dropped his hands, balling them into fists by his side.

'Darcie Lock.' He said the name without emotion – a greeting of sorts.

'Hugo,' she whispered.

He walked straight on, disappearing into the kitchen. Darcie sprang away from the wall, wanting to be long gone when he came back. She ran through the hall and out into the sunshine. The forecourt was full of vans. She almost bumped into a man with a sniffer dog on a lead, half stumbled down the steps, and made a dash for the cliff path. She didn't stop until she reached the bottom of the steep wooden steps leading down to the private cove. The tide was in, leaving only a little fringe of sand for her to stand on. She leaned forward, retching on to the flyblown seaweed.

Hugo Kraus walked back up the corridor slowly, balancing a tray of tea. He passed the spot where he'd met her. The tray rattled and tea sloshed over the rims of the mugs. She'd gone. Of course. He remembered how scared she had looked, like she had in the Country Club in Nairobi, backed up against the changing room wall. That was before she kneed him in the groin and tied him up. He wasn't fooled.

'Nice to see you too, Darcie,' he muttered to the air.

What was he going to do about her now? he wondered as he handed the tea round to the techie guys laying out the extra surveillance equipment.

When Mrs Smith had told him that Darcie was here – that he was to keep his distance – he had laughed in her face. It was a sick joke.

'Is this some kind of test for me?' he'd asked. 'To see if I can behave?'

Mrs Smith had frowned. 'I wouldn't expose Darcie to you if I had a choice. No, it is not a test, it is an order: keep away.'

'Yes, ma'am.'

He'd forgotten how small Darcie was compared to him, but that had always been her advantage: no one ever expected her to have the guts to defend herself. And she was obviously terrified of him. Good. Let him be her problem – he wasn't about to allow her to become his. He would ignore the fact that she was there – act as normal. Wait.

'Oi, lad, this has sugar in it!' One of the engineers gave an exaggerated grimace.

Hugo snapped back to the present. 'Yeah, three with, four without.'

'No, son, it was two and five. Brain with the retention capacity of a goldfish, have you?' The other men chuckled.

'Yeah, sorry,' mumbled Hugo, taking the cup. 'I'll fix her – I mean, it.'

. . .

The long black limousine carrying the secretary general to the United Nations turned into the drive of St Helen's House. Carmen Lopez had requested that she arrive at the venue a day ahead of the delegations. If she was to head up the conference properly, she wanted to feel like a hostess; know her way around; be at home. Looking up from her briefing papers, she saw the building appear at the end of the winding road like a castle out of Don Quixote. She fell in love with it instantly – its proud old grey stone walls set against the green sweep of the cliff top and the blue of the sea. The UN flag rippled over the archway in her honour next to the Union Jack. Charming.

The conference organiser was waiting to greet her. John Riddell had sent her the best: his own private secretary, James Harlem. Foreign Secretary Riddell would be joining them later in the evening.

The young man sprang forward to open her door, his auburn hair blowing messily in the breeze. 'Good afternoon, Secretary General. How was your journey?'

'Fine, thank you, James. How's Baby Leo and Marianne?'

'Flourishing.'

'I hope you have lots of photos to show me?'

'Of course.' He smiled with pride and patted his breast pocket.

'Everything ready?'

'We're just putting the finishing touches to it all now.' James directed her into the entrance hall.

'You're not to worry: hosting a conference is child's play compared to the early days of parenthood. Look on it as a chance to catch up with your sleep.'

He laughed. 'Where would you like to dine tonight, ma'am? In the hall or privately in your room?'

'Oh, I'll dine with the team. It will be a chance for us to get to know each other before our guests arrive.' She flashed one of her perfect smiles at him, smoothing her long black hair over a shoulder. At fifty-five, she still didn't have a grey hair on her head, at least not that she let anyone see. It was all part of the identity she had patiently constructed for herself. The youngest ever president of Bolivia, serving two full terms, now the head of the United Nations – good going for a girl originally from the slums.

James glowed in the sunlight of her attention. 'I'm sure we'd all like that, ma'am.'

'So, James, who is here already?'

'Most of the protection people – apart from the

ones meeting our guests at Bristol airport, of course. The staff. That's it. Everyone else has cleared out.'

'Can I have a list? I always think it important to notice the backroom people – it can make a huge difference to the success or otherwise of these events.'

'Of course.' He passed her a list from his file.

She ran her finger down the names, pausing at the bottom. 'Good. I'll tour the conference room itself before dinner and then we can take a breath before the plunge tomorrow.'

'Shall I show you your room now?'

'That can wait. I think I'll stretch my legs before it gets dark. I've been sitting in planes or cars for the last eighteen hours. Any suggestions?'

James nodded. 'That path there – it'll take you down to the sea.'

Carmen sauntered out into the open air, followed at a discreet distance by her protection officer. It felt good to be free of responsibility for a few moments. She made a point of stealing time for herself every day so she wouldn't forget who and what she really was: a girl – grown up now but still an ordinary girl who liked to feel sand between her toes.

James had been right: the little cove looked absolutely perfect for a private stroll. Carmen edged her way carefully down the steep steps, fearful of taking a spill. She smiled sourly as she thought of the headlines . . .

'Calamity Carmen!'
  'Secretary General falls at first hurdle.'

Her life had become a series of newspaper stories. It seemed a long time since she earned a pittance selling the Correo on street corners, before she had even decided to become a journalist. Now she was filling their pages with stories of her exploits. She found it bemusing when, like now, she stopped to think about the course her life had taken.

She dropped to the sand and walked to the water's edge. The tide was going out – the sand brushed smooth, studded with shells and pebbles. Unable to repress a childlike instinct to collect, she picked up a bright pink stone and slid it into her pocket. She hopped out of her Jimmy Choo sandals and let the cold water lick her toes: delicious.

It was then she noticed the newly made foot-prints ahead of her. So her cove was not deserted after all.

Robinson Crusoe now, she thought with a smile. Shading her eyes against the slanting rays of the setting sun, she saw someone – a girl – sitting on a rock surrounded by water. She was fully clothed but it looked as though she had swum there. Carmen's maternal instinct clicked into play: her own daughter was not much older than this child. She waved.

'Are you all right? Are you stuck?'

The girl looked up, her face streaked with tears. 'I'm fine.'

'You don't look fine to me.'

The girl slid from the rock and into the water: it only came up to her thighs. She held her arms out. 'See, I'm fine.' She began wading back to shore.

'You're a bit wet.' Carmen frowned at the damp school uniform. 'You'll catch cold. What will your mother say?'

The girl began to laugh. 'I think she'll say it's the least of my worries right now.'

Carmen clucked her tongue sympathetically. She remembered what it was like to be a teenager. It had to be a boy: what else at this girl's age? 'Where are you staying? I can get someone to give you a lift back.'

'No, I'm fine –'

'If you say you're fine once more . . .' Carmen paused, waiting for her to fill the gap.

'Darcie,' the girl supplied reluctantly.

'. . . Darcie, then I'll scream. I will. You don't believe me?' Carmen put her hands on her hips.

Darcie shook her head, unable to stop a smile coming as this woman in an expensive business suit threatened to let rip. 'I'm fine.'

'That's it.' The Secretary General of the United Nations threw back her head and screamed. Darcie stared at her in astonishment, then found herself thrown on the sand with a knee on her back.

'Santa Maria! Let her up, Brian!' Carmen ordered the protection officer who had hurtled out of nowhere to disarm her 'attacker'. 'I'm so sorry, Darcie.'

But Darcie was shaking, not with fear, but with laughter. She'd just worked out who this woman was with her oh-so-familiar face and her police escort. She turned on her back and giggled helplessly at the red-faced officer and the South American woman who had screamed like a banshee to cheer her up.

Carmen extended a hand and pulled her to her feet. 'Better now?'

'Yes, ma'am.'

'Brian, can you get someone to drive Darcie home, please?'

'Really, there's no need. I'm staying just up there. St Helen's.'

'You look a bit young to be on the staff,' observed Carmen. 'Do your parents work here?'

'No, I'm a student. Please, don't worry about me; I've been told to keep out of your way.'

The secretary general smiled. 'Not doing a very good job of that, are you?'

Darcie looked down at her soggy clothing, aware she was blushing. 'I s'pose not.'

Carmen lightly caressed her cheek in a maternal gesture – for the South American, touch was a natural part of her behaviour, a means to break down barriers between people. 'It is a good thing too, Darcie. Otherwise I might never have met you and had this chance to profoundly embarrass myself. One dose of humiliation a day is good for the soul. And now, I really must insist you change out of those wet things.'

'Yes, ma'am.' Darcie gave her a wobbly salute and bounded up the steps ahead of them.

'Sorry about that, ma'am,' muttered Brian sheepishly.

Secretary General Lopez waved away the apology. 'It was not your fault. I promise you next time I scream like that, it won't be a false alarm.'

Drying off in her room, Darcie couldn't help smiling every time she thought of Carmen Lopez. She did not conform at all to the stereotype of world leaders – but then, that was her secret, according to the press. A meeting with her might end up at a salsa bar or strolling along the boardwalk in the moonlight. Her theory – and she had gone on record numerous times saying as much – was that if you made politicians feel human, then they would start to act like one. If anyone was going to make headway over an intractable problem like Tazbekistan, it would be Carmen Lopez.

Darcie stood at her window, towelling her hair dry, watching the comings and goings in the courtyard below. More people were arriving, carrying boxes of briefing papers and equipment. A florist from Truro drew up and began unloading flower arrangements. Like a giant bee after nectar, a policeman probed each one with a wand-shaped detector before allowing them inside. Despite the seriousness of the preparations, everyone was smiling. The Carmen feel-good factor was spreading. The next few days might be really enjoyable, thought Darcie, if it wasn't for the presence of Hugo Kraus.

The physical sickness she had experienced on first seeing him had passed but the very thought of him still made her squirm. He was like a nightmare monster from childhood – the kind you were convinced hid under the bed or in the cupboard – making you too afraid to move around your own house. In an effort to control her wayward emotions, Darcie tried to rationalise what she felt. Of course, it was natural to be scared of a boy who had attempted to kill her. But what could he do now? He had no reason to harm her – in fact, every reason to leave her alone. And yet . . .

Someone tapped gently on the door.

'Who is it?' Darcie asked, her heart thumping. It couldn't be him, surely?

'May I come in?'

She felt immediate relief when she realised that it was Gladys Smith. 'Of course.'

Darcie unlocked the door and stood back. Gladys entered, giving the room a quick inspection, as was her custom when entering unknown territory.

'Very nice. My room is on the floor below if you need me. You have a better view though.'

Darcie shook out her wet shirt and hung it on a hanger at the window. She was wearing a bathrobe provided by St Helen's – all her clothes being soaked through.

'I've sent for your things,' Gladys continued, 'but I'm afraid Mr and Mrs Galt are not being very helpful.'

'Oh?' Darcie was surprised – this seemed very out of character. 'Should I call them to explain?'

'I don't think that will help.' Gladys decided not to tell her about the unpleasant rumours doing the rounds of Truro about their son. 'I'll drop by to see them tonight on my way to London.'

'So you're not staying?' Darcie wasn't proud that her voice betrayed her fear. For all her coldness, at least Mrs Smith understood the history between Darcie and Hugo and represented some sort of buffer between them. Darcie felt even less comfortable knowing that was going to be taken away.

'Only for a few days. I would have been long gone already if it had not been for the little detour via your school this morning. I have to make myself scarce during this conference – my room is needed as a communications centre.'

'Oh, I see.'

'I did get you these though to tide you over.' She placed on the bed a clean T-shirt with the St Helen's logo, a zipped jacket, underwear and fatigue trousers. 'You can get more from the housekeeper – we keep a stock for our students – probably a bit on the large side for you but better than your school uniform.'

'Thanks.' Darcie wondered if Mrs Smith was going to ask her how she got wet. Or perhaps she already knew?

The SIS officer moved to the window and gazed down on the forecourt. 'So you met Hugo?'

Darcie nodded, not trusting herself to make further comment.

'He was civil, I hope?'

'We barely spoke to each other.'

'Good. I'm sorry it had to happen like this, but now it has, I hope you both make the best of it.'

Scrunching the towel in her hands, Darcie mimed wringing Mrs Smith's neck. 'You're joking, right?'

'Darcie, you are an SIS agent, like it or not.' Gladys held up her hand to stop Darcie interrupting. 'I know you don't want to admit it but ask yourself why you are here, being protected by us?'

Darcie's urge to protest subsided, knowing she was on very shaky ground as long as she continued to rely on this particular band of protectors. It was easier to be her own person when she was with her parents – but, here and now, it felt like she was the property of SIS.

'In that case,' Mrs Smith continued, seeing her point had sunk in, 'you should take the opportunity to learn to face your fear. Do you know how many people I've had to confront knowing full well they would prefer me dead? I've lost count. Half the job is pretending to your enemy that you are his best friend. How else do you think we find things out? What do you think your father and mother had to do all that time you were living in Nairobi?'

Darcie slumped on the bed. 'I understand – really I do – but you must all be tougher than me. I don't feel ready for this –'

'No one ever feels ready.'

'Any tips then?' Darcie knew her tone was sarcastic but she couldn't help herself.

'Smile, keep your thoughts to yourself, and

remember that you beat him – that always helps. After all, he's only one boy.'

'He's a monster.'

'I've met very few monsters in my time and I can tell you that Hugo is not one of them. He's damaged.'

'If you say so – but me being here is not going to help him.'

'Have you not asked yourself whether it might be harder for him to face you than for you to face him?'

'I can't believe that.'

'Think about it.'

When Gladys left, Darcie pulled on the clean clothes, considering what she had said. Was it true that Hugo was in some way scared of her? Highly unlikely. She checked her watch. Somewhere along the way she had forgotten to eat lunch and was now starving. As if in answer to her hunger, a gong sounded down in the entrance hall. If she wanted to have dinner, she'd have to face Hugo again. But then Carmen would be there too – that alone was worth the trip downstairs. Gathering her courage, she left the safe haven of her room in search of food.

The dining room was in the great hall of the castle – an arched roof and minstrels' gallery at the far end, long trestle tables like something out of

Hogwarts. There was a cold stone scent to the air, the kind of smell that hung around in old churches. Darcie was one of the first to arrive. As it was an informal meal, Kito Bridges and his staff were serving tonight from a mobile canteen along one wall, the modern equipment and halogen lights jarring with the ancient surroundings. She grabbed a plate and joined the queue.

'Honey-glazed carrots?' asked Kito as she reached the vegetables.

'Please.'

Kito ladled a generous spoonful next to the chicken. 'My son said you were misbehavin' this morning – jumped out of the window during a lesson.'

'Oh, yes, about that –'

'How are the teeth?'

'What?' 'He said you went to the dentist and didn't come back.'

'Er, yes, there was a change of plan. I'm staying here now.'

Kito raised an eyebrow but merely waved her along. 'If you're not busy tonight, Jake's coming to help me with preparations for tomorrow's banquet.'

'When?' Darcie asked, almost dropping her tray

as she made an unwise attempt to look at her watch. She juggled it steady.

'Half eight. When we've finished up here.'

'Great! I'll come and find him then.'

Darcie took a seat at the end of one table, still grinning to herself. Jake would be here tonight: it was better than she could have hoped. More at ease, she barely jumped when someone touched her lightly on the back.

'Happier, Darcie?' asked Carmen softly.

'Yes, much,' she nodded.

'Good. How's the food?'

'Very nice.'

'Excellent. See you later.'

Carmen joined the queue with everyone else and was soon chatting to Kito, Josephine and the other kitchen staff as if she'd known them all her life. Kito nodded in Darcie's direction once, causing Carmen to turn and smile at her. Darcie blushed, guessing what was being discussed. She kept her eyes fixed on her plate, trying to ignore the fact that her ears were burning. When she thought it safe to look up again, she found that Carmen was sitting on the far table among the technicians. Hugo was with them, listening seriously to everything that was said as if his life depended on it. One man cracked a joke, provoking a great bellow of laughter that caused a momentary pause in the hubbub as all turned to see what was going on. Carmen was smiling too but she seemed concerned that Hugo was not joining in the merriment; she even reached out at one point and patted his arm. Darcie felt an irrational twinge of jealousy. She'd known that Carmen was famous for her ability to make everyone feel special – but Hugo?

Get a grip, Darcie, she chided herself. You can't seriously feel jealous of Hugo.

Darcie remained isolated at the end of her table, watching the comings and goings with detached interest. She was just wondering how she was going to pass the time until eight thirty when Carmen arrived at her shoulder again, on this occasion with a reluctant Hugo in tow.

'Darcie, do you know Hugo?' she asked innocently.

Darcie gulped. 'We've met.'

'Hugo tells me he's also staying here. I thought, as the only two young people, you could be company for each other during the conference.' Carmen paused, expecting the two of them to say something. 'Go on, don't be shy. Hugo, why don't you take Darcie for a coffee? They're serving it in the library.'

Darcie was rapidly revising her opinion of

Carmen's interpersonal skills: she now seemed like some nightmare mother pushing two stranger children together at a party with the promise that they'd be great friends or, perhaps more appropriately, like a dog owner swearing to a visitor that his snarling pet Rottweiler was really a sweetheart when you got to know him.

'It's all right, Ms Lopez, Hugo and I, well, we actually . . .' Darcie floundered for an explanation: 'hate each other's guts' seemed melodramatic even if it happened to be true.

But then Hugo surprised her by interrupting. 'Do you take your coffee white or black, Darcie?'

'That's more like it!' Carmen hoisted Darcie up by the elbow and whispered in her ear. 'Take a word of advice from me: it's better when you have boy-trouble to let him see you around other men. It'll do Jake good.'

Darcie could only stare. The fact that Carmen was so well briefed on her private life was not as disturbing as the insinuation that she could be romantically attached to Hugo in anyone's head.

'Go on,' chided Carmen, 'don't keep Hugo waiting. Ah, James, any sign of the minister?'

She had turned to other matters, now talking animatedly to John Riddell's private secretary.

'He's been held up, ma'am. Last minute problem in London,' explained James, ushering her away. 'I'd better fill you in.'

Westminster, London: Skies clouding overnight, cool, 14°C

Foreign Secretary John Riddell was currently closeted away with Christopher Lock and his senior advisers in the Locarno room in the Foreign Office. A Victorian extravaganza in gilt and red, the room looked out over a vast covered courtyard – a white marble expanse called the Durbar Court, a relic of the days when these offices ran India and the rest of the British Empire. The men gathered around the table now only managed the fading influence of Great Britain, and right now that was seriously under threat.

'Christopher, what do you mean, "you advise we call off the conference"? The delegates are in the air as we speak – the secretary general is at St Helen's – it's too late to call it off!' John Riddell tapped his papers irritably with his fountain pen, spraying ink over the 'top secret' stamp on the cover.

Christopher sighed, knowing he'd have to repeat himself several times before his point was taken on board – which looked unlikely in view of the foreign secretary's attitude. The ornate clock ticked solemnly on the mantelpiece, its disapproving face set at twenty past seven in a drooping moustache.

'As you will see from your brief, sir, I've had late – but what I consider reliable – information from Russian intelligence that suggests that there's a serious problem in the Tazbek delegation. The military adviser, General Yerdan Paschuk, has argued with his colleagues and we think he is only coming to disrupt the conference. I advise extreme caution.'

'Extreme caution? What does that mean exactly?' Riddell asked irritably.

'The chance of failure is high. If you go ahead, I suggest you send a junior minister to lessen the political fallout.' Christopher kept his face bland as he assessed the foreign secretary's reaction. Riddell surely would not want to be the one with egg on his face when the Russians and Tazbeks descended to a punch-up over the conference table.

But he was wrong: Riddell had more ethics than most politicians, placing loyalty over his own political future. 'I can't do that; it would be an insult to Ms Lopez.'

'Then I suggest you give her a gentle warning – obviously without revealing the source mentioned in the briefing I had prepared for you.'

John Riddell gazed around at the guarded expressions on his advisers' faces, seeking some guidance. Finding none, he strode to the French windows opening out onto a balcony overlooking the courtyard. The glow of computer screens could be seen in the office windows flanking the space – the civil servants were all working late, preparing for the spotlight of international attention that would be focused on the conference. It would be a huge humiliation to pull out at this stage.

'I can't leave the secretary general to face a crumbling conference on her own,' he said at last. 'And if I did pull out, that would be used as the reason why it failed so we'd get an even worse press. I'll worry about the politics; you keep an eye on the Tazbeks.'

'Very good, sir. If you think best.'

'But you disagree?' Riddell could hardly hide his frustration with his secret service advisers – they were always so obtuse: refusing to call a spade a spade, instead claiming that any information on hand-held implements was on a strict 'need-to-know' basis.

Christopher closed his file and locked it in his briefcase. 'It's your call, sir.'

'But you think I've made the wrong one?' Riddell pressed him for a straight answer.

The director of special operations got to his feet. 'The risks are not only political. According to the Russians' informant, Paschuk is not the sanest of individuals. There are rumours he is planning to do something drastic.'

'But he is isolated in the delegation you say – fallen out with the rest?'

'True.'

'So he may still be sidelined?'

'He is very hard to sideline – he controls the security forces in Tazbekistan. He is the muscle – his colleagues merely the brains.'

'Then it's about time the brains took over. These men of violence like Paschuk have led Tazbekistan up a blind alley. This conference is the best chance the Tazbeks have of retreating with dignity.' Riddell patted his pockets for his cigarettes, then remembered he'd given up. 'The people will back their leaders if they see how much they stand to gain if they choose a peaceful solution with the Russians; and I sincerely hope they realise how much they have to lose if they continue on the present course.'

Convincing himself with this little speech, Riddell turned to a junior official. 'Have the car brought round, please, Marjorie. The rest of you, I'd like you to prepare a defensive line for the press if things do go pear-shaped thanks to General Paschuk. Christopher, regular updates please.'

'Of course, sir. And good luck.' Christopher held out his palm.

'You think I'll need it?' Riddell shook his hand in farewell.

'If you want an honest answer, yes, I do. A great deal of it.'

Riddell quit the room for the first time feeling really worried. A straight answer from Christopher Lock! That was both unprecedented and disturbing.

St Helen's, Cornwall: Approaching cold front, showers likely, 13°C

Darcie followed Hugo out of the hall towards the library, wondering what was going on inside his square-shaped head. It was strange: in a superficial way he shared some similarities with Stingo – same colouring, soldier's haircut and strong build, though Hugo was already taller – but in all the essentials he was the opposite: selfish, violent and completely without a sense of humour. He was sweating despite it being a cool evening – she could see his shirt clinging to his shoulder blades. Perhaps Mrs Smith had been right – perhaps he was afraid of her? Finding that Carmen was no longer watching them, Darcie made to peel off from Hugo and return to her room.

'Wait!' he called, catching her arm then quickly dropping it as if burned.

'I've got nothing to say to you, Hugo,' Darcie said firmly, continuing towards the stairs.

'No, please.' The word came with difficulty. 'I've something I want to ask you.' Hugo was looking very shifty, checking who could see them. 'Look, just come in for a moment and grab a quick coffee – I won't keep you.'

Darcie paused, then nodded. She didn't want him pursuing her up the stairs and out of sight of other people. Stingo would never forgive her if she were foolish enough to let Hugo Kraus of all people get her on her own.

Hugo swooped on the table laid out with coffee and shoved a small cup and saucer into her hand. He then took one for himself but put it down when he noticed it rattling in his grip. Darcie sipped hers with a steady hand. The more fidgety he was, the easier it became for her to pretend she wasn't scared.

'Look, Darcie.' Hugo ran his hands over his hair nervously. 'I know you owe me nothing, but I'm trying to make a new start here – I'm doing well, I think – and I just want to ask you to keep what happened in Kenya to yourself.'

'Why should I do that?' Darcie stared frostily at him, remembering how all the girls in her year at school had found him attractive. She only saw a predator: the boy who had shot Stingo in the leg and sent her off to be fed to the lions.

'I suppose because you're a lot nicer than I am?' He tried to smile but it was a miserable failure. 'There are people here I respect – but they know nothing about my past. Agent Smith promised me a new start.'

'So?'

Darcie could tell he was getting angry. His cheeks were flushed red and, though he probably didn't realise it, he was pulverising a sugar cube in his left hand.

'So I'm asking you to help me make the break – not drag up the Nairobi stuff.'

This felt like a dream – or one of those conversations she'd rehearsed in her head after the explosion at the country club had left her confined to a wheelchair for six weeks.

'Are you saying you're sorry?' she asked. Her tone was terse – Gladys Smith would have been proud.

Hugo glanced over her shoulder, flicking sugar on to the floor as he brushed his hand on his trouser leg. 'I will if you like.'

So he hadn't changed then. 'It's not what I want that matters – not if you don't mean it. You're not the least bit sorry you tried to kill me, are you?'

He shrugged. 'It was never anything personal – you just got in the way.'

'Don't kid yourself – I seem to remember it got very personal at the end. You make me sick, Hugo.' She slammed the cup on the table and marched out of the room, heading towards the kitchens, anger making her blood thunder in her ears.

Hugo caught up with her in the corridor. 'OK, OK, I'm sorry! Is that what you want?'

'You don't get it, do you?' Darcie resisted the urge to scream, keeping her tone even. 'It means nothing because you'd do the same all over again. You shouldn't even be here – you should be in jail, locked up, as far away from me as possible!'

Glowering at her, Hugo opened his mouth to say something when Jake stepped between them.

'You all right, Darcie?' Jake asked, putting his arm around her shoulders. He could feel her trembling. 'Who's this?' He jerked his head at Hugo. Though Hugo topped him by a head, Jake looked ready to take him on for her.

'No one,' Darcie replied.

Hugo swore and walked off, banging the door behind him.

'No one?' Jake looked at her quizzically. 'So what was all that about wanting to chuck him in jail?'

'Nothing – he's just someone I used to know from before.'

'From before what?'

Darcie didn't have an answer so she buried her face in Jake's collar, breathing in his normality, so far removed from the chaos of her life. The fact that he was so grounded in Truro, had a great family, grown up with the same friends for years, was probably part of her attraction to him. Added to that, he made her laugh. He couldn't be more perfect for her really.

'Forget it. Jake, it's so good to see you.'

He hugged her back, unconsciously nuzzling the top of her head. 'Good to see you too. So what's going on?'

'It's complicated.'

Jake steered her into the kitchen, running the gauntlet of curious looks from Josephine and his dad, and out into the backyard. He pulled her on to a bench beside the wheelie bins.

'Very romantic,' Darcie said, sniffing the sour smell of last week's rubbish.

'Yeah, well, you know me. Anyway, who said anything about us being romantic?' Jake put his arm around her shoulders and let her lean against him.

Darcie bit her lip, knowing that her thoughts had run away with her. She snuggled up to him, deciding not to answer.

'So, are you going to tell me what's going on?' Jake asked after a pause. He stroked her arm.

'You wouldn't believe me if I told you.' Darcie decided then that if he asked her why, she'd tell him everything.

Jake dropped his hand from her hair. She could feel his body tense. 'Is it because you think I'd be angry?'

'Maybe, I dunno.' Darcie considered her recent history, trying to imagine what he would make of the tale. 'I think I'm more scared that you'll think I'm making it all up.'

Jake gently removed his arm from her shoulder.

She sat up straight. Now they were sitting side by side, barely touching.

Jake cleared his throat, his embarrassment obvious. 'There's this rumour, y'know.'

'Rumour?' Darcie wondered what bit of her chequered past had surfaced in Truro.

'Yeah, something about you and that SAS guy.'

Her heart sank, feeling the fragile threads of affection woven between them beginning to snap. 'I don't understand what you mean.'

'The head sort of gave a speech after you jumped out of the window –'

'Oh, great,' Darcie said in a hollow tone.

Jake now looked angry, his hands clenched on his thighs. 'Told us that you and Ken Galt aren't really related, and that you might've run off together. Said the police were looking for you to take you back to your mum. He said we should tell them if we know where you are.'

Darcie felt a jolt of alarm. 'But you didn't, did you?'

'No. I wanted to talk to you first. Is it true?'

This was horrible. She now understood why Marcus and Claire had not wanted to cooperate over her stuff – they must be mad at her for dragging their son's name through the mud. 'No, none of it's true. Stingo's been a good friend. Really, he's more of a bodyguard, an older brother,' she shook her head, 'definitely not a boyfriend.'

Jake got up and began kicking the bin mindlessly, making it clang against the wall behind. 'Bodyguard. Funny fantasy life you lead, Darcie.' His tone was bitter.

'I knew you wouldn't believe me.' Darcie hugged her knees to her chest.

Jake rounded on her, letting his anger show. 'And what about your mum? Don't you care that she's worried about you?'

'What?'

'The American guy said she was fighting to get you back to the States, trying to save you.'

'That's not true. Mum doesn't want me there – she knows it's not safe.'

'That's not what the lawyer said.'

'Yeah, well, maybe he's got other reasons for saying that.'

They had reached a silence that seemed impossible to break. Darcie felt like a swimmer caught in a rip tide, dragged further from the place she wanted to be despite all efforts to reach it. How could she explain that the American president wanted her out of the way? Jake would never believe her. No one

would believe her. They would think she was para-
noid or mad.

Jake scrubbed his hand over his face in a frustrated gesture. 'Darcie, look, I . . . I suppose I'd
better go and help Dad.' With an abruptness that felt
final, he disappeared into the kitchen without saying
goodbye.

So that was it. Darcie stared at the door Jake had
gone through, wishing it would open and they could
run that conversation again – do it right. Why did
this always have to happen to her? As soon as she
got close to someone, it was finished.

Why?

Because she'd got mixed up with spies – because
she'd been born one, thanks to her parents' choices,
not hers. Each new start she made had been spoiled
– she'd never escape, never get rid of her past. Lies
and rumours always followed her because she
couldn't risk telling anyone the truth.

Not wanting to pass through the kitchen, she
tried the gate – locked. Deciding on a less conventional route, she climbed on to the wheelie bin and
dropped down on the other side of the fence. At first
she didn't recognize where she was, then found her
bearings from the car park. A black car had just
purred to a stop and a chauffeur was unloading bags.

Over by the front entrance, Carmen was greeting a man enthusiastically while officials gathered in a huddle on the bottom steps.

Darcie turned her back on the reception party and made for the gardens. They raked steeply down to the sea: terraces of exotic plants protected by the Cornish micro-climate, now in their late autumn bloom. She soon found what she wanted: an enclosed area surrounding a fountain, dark with yew hedges, highlighted by white marble statues. It felt private.

She lay on her back on the lawn, looking at the stars, trying to ignore the fact that she was crying. She let the tears trickle down her face, into her hair, eventually reaching the grass. Little night insects hummed around her, attracted by the salt trails on her cheeks. Memories of the fun she'd had with Jake over the past few weeks flitted through her mind like moths: listening to music together curled up on a sofa, kicking a ball around at school, clowning around in the corridors. He'd helped her ease into her new life, accepting her silence about the past with a shrug that said he was prepared to wait for her to tell him more when she was ready. But the rumours that she was into something dangerous had pushed his easy-going nature too far. She couldn't blame him: it was hard to be with a person who was hiding so much from everyone – look at her and her parents, how their secrets had made her suffer!

She found her thoughts turning to what Hugo had asked her. He'd wanted to make a new start and she'd thrown the past in his face and run, much as Jake had from her. What had she wanted? Hugo to come weeping to her on his knees, begging her forgiveness? What purpose would that have served? Could she have actually done Hugo some good by promising to let him leave his crimes behind him? Maybe he was becoming a better person.

Maybe he wasn't.

What did it matter? He wasn't her responsibility. But if she could help him, she owed it to herself to do so. After one of the worst days of her life, it would make her feel better at the very least. She wouldn't then have to blame herself if he went off the rails again.

Decision made, Darcie got up and returned to the house. She scouted the ground-floor rooms, trying to spot him among the visitors. Tall men in suits, interspersed with the occasional smartly dressed woman, were gathered in the library for coffee. Failing to locate Hugo among them, she checked the room plan at the reception – neither her name nor his were listed. It appeared they did not officially exist.

Could it wait till morning? Darcie knew herself well enough to realise that this new, wiser mood would fade overnight. She had to do it now before the moment passed. Taking another approach, she checked the list against the floor plans and found two rooms on the top floor unallocated – her own and one only a few doors away. That had to be Hugo's. She ran up the backstairs, arriving breathless outside it. She paused to listen; there was someone moving around inside. As she raised her hand to knock, she almost changed her mind.

Forcing her hand, she rapped twice.

The door opened and Hugo stood before her, wrapped only in a towel.

'Oh, er, sorry. I didn't mean to get you out of the bath.' Darcie's gaze dropped to his toes. She hadn't noticed them before – they were big and square. Trust Hugo to have rugged toes. He also had something strapped to his ankle – a tag.

He took a step back, hiding it from sight behind the door. 'Doesn't matter. What do you want?' No longer blocking the light, Hugo now noticed that she was covered in grass and smudges of dirt; she looked like she'd been crying. 'Are you all right? Not ill or something?'

Darcie gave a hiccup of laughter. Hugo, worrying about her welfare. There had to be a first time for everything.

'No, I'm fine.' She wiped her wrist across her face. 'I've been thinking about what you asked me and I . . . er . . .' He was watching her with that cold look of his – the one that made her want to run a mile. 'I think I understand. So I just wanted to say that I won't tell anyone about what happened before – you get your new start. Just forget I'm here.'

Hugo dropped his shoulders, that small gesture revealing how tense he had been talking to her. 'Thanks, Darcie.' He held out a hand. 'Deal?'

She looked down at his palm for a moment, then shook it, suppressing a shudder.

'Deal.' She released his hand quickly and turned to go. 'It doesn't mean I've forgotten though.'

He gave her his wolfish smile. 'Neither have I. See you around, Darcie Lock.'

[6]

The following morning, Darcie woke to find a note had been pushed under her door during the night. It was from Jake.

Darcie, Sorry I was such an idiot but I'm a bit confused about everything. I won't tell anyone where you are if you don't want me to but I can't help worrying about you. Dad said that this place is very private – only for VIPs – and he can't imagine what you're doing here. Aunt Josephine thinks you might need help . . .

Darcie's toes curled at the thought that her situation had been discussed so freely by all the kitchen staff. She wasn't sure she could face them again . . .

But that doesn't matter for now. What I wanted

to tell you is that I'm still here for you if you need me. Call me. Jake

Darcie folded the letter and slipped it inside her trouser pocket. Now all the cooks would be watching her every move, speculating about her mental state. She took out her phone, wondering if she should ring him. Frankly, she didn't feel like talking to him just now – there was nothing she could say to make him understand, so what was the point? She looked up his number in her address book but didn't press 'call'. Then her eyes alighted on Stingo's entry. He'd always been there for her; it would take more than a rumour to push him away.

The phone was picked up at once.

'Darcie, why the hell are you calling me?' Stingo sounded both furtive and angry. 'I told you only to ring me in an emergency.'

''Cause I needed . . . never mind. Sorry.' Darcie made to end the call.

'No, no, I'm sorry,' Stingo jumped in quickly. 'Don't hang up. I wasn't thinking. It's just that I'm in a lot of trouble right now and you shouldn't really get in touch with me.'

'I know – the rumour.'

'Yeah. Only my squad knows the truth – thank

God; they'd kill me if they thought I'd done something like that.'

It was a relief to know that his team was standing
by him. 'So what's happening?'

'Look, it's not your fault, but I'm being investi-
gated by the military police. They haven't got a shred
of a case, just accusations, but they have to go
through the motions. Unfortunately, it's not helped
that our jaunt from Egypt wasn't exactly legit!'

Darcie moved to the window. Rain clouds were
beating in from the west – good weather for the
allotment. 'Your mum and dad are angry with me.'

'Yeah, they probably are, but it's not really about
you, you must know that. I think they're ashamed.
Truro's a small place and gossip like this has the
habit of taking root. Don't worry about me or them –
we can handle it. I'm not too worried if my super-
hero status takes a nosedive.'

Darcie wasn't convinced. A few weeks back, he'd
gone into the desert to drag her out at great personal
risk; she'd repaid him by bringing this upon him.
'Can I do anything to help – call someone?'

She could hear Stingo sigh; she imagined him
rubbing his big, square hands over his short hair in
frustration. 'The people here might ask to speak to
you but I doubt the spooks will let them. Probably

just as well – they have no evidence of anything; we don't want to give them the chance to twist your words. But really, don't worry. Your dad's trying to help; he'll sort it out.'

'Good. I'm glad he's doing that.' Her father would know what to do. At least someone in her family was trying to improve the situation for him.

'And how are you?' Stingo made an effort to change the subject.

'Do you want the truth?' 'Course I do, Zebra.'

The use of her nickname among Stingo's SAS mates made her miss them all acutely – she'd been adopted as their unlucky mascot and they had looked after her like one of their own. She leaned against the windowsill.

'Pretty rubbish if you must know. My new friends at school all think I'm some kind of weirdo kid gone wrong. I don't think it helped that the last they saw of me was when I escaped from the classroom through the window. They probably all think I've ended up in rehab.'

'Yeah, well, that wouldn't be very reassuring.' He sounded like he was smiling.

Darcie steeled herself as she anticipated how he was going to react to the next snippet of information. She tried to keep her tone light. 'Then I pitch up at this place and find that Mrs Smith has seen fit to park Hugo Kraus here.'

'What!' The line crackled as if Stingo had dropped the phone. He juggled it back into position again. 'You're joking, right?'

'That's what I said.'

'Darcie, get out of there.'

'And go where exactly? Anyway, Hugo and I have reached a sort of truce, I think.'

'Don't trust him – never trust him! I know him, remember. He's got unfinished business with you, I'm sure of it.'

'Do you really think I need the warning?'

She heard him curse under his breath. 'No, probably not. All the same, what's he doing at St Helen's of all places?'

'Training with our friends. He's making a new start.'

'He should be in jail.'

'Yeah, that's what I told him.' They shared a moment of silence. 'So,' Darcie asked with false brightness, 'whose shoes would you rather be in right now: yours or mine?'

'Tough choice,' laughed Stingo. 'Mind you, if I were there, I'd enjoy taking Kraus apart bit by bit.

My leg's still playing up thanks to the bullet he put in it.'

'I wouldn't advise it, even for you. He's bigger and meaner than ever.'

'Another reason if you needed it to keep your distance then.'

'I'll try – as long as the secretary general doesn't keep on throwing us together like a desperate matchmaker.'

'And I've always rated her – a good-looking woman and smart.'

'But dumb when it comes to Hugo and me.'

'Keep in touch.'

'I will.'

The call may have been unwise but Darcie felt much better having spoken to Stingo. It was perhaps a sign of how odd her life had become that her best mate was a soldier a good decade older than her, but all things considered, she couldn't regret the last few months because they had given her the gift of Stingo's friendship.

Dressing quickly, she dashed down the stairs fully intending to grab some breakfast and disappear somewhere for the day; but before she could reach the hall, a middle-aged lady with short, white-blonde hair stepped in her path.

'Miss Lock?'

'Yes?'

'I'm Marjorie Jefferson, the housekeeper. Mrs Smith left me instructions to keep an eye on you this week while she's away.'

'I'll try not to be any bother.' Darcie attempted to dodge past but Mrs Jefferson hadn't finished.

'Well, then. We've not been able to fix you up with a tutor at such short notice – what with the conference and everything –'

'You must be very busy.'

Mrs Jefferson smiled at her blatant attempts to escape. 'Yes, I am, but not too busy to think about your needs. Mrs Smith said you are a very special girl and asked me to treat you accordingly. Now, there's a gym and a pool down in the basement that you are welcome to use. Mrs Smith has left some schoolwork that you can do in my room. I've put you in there with Mr Kraus who's also staying with us. Have you met him?'

Darcie nodded. Why was everyone trying to throw them together?

'All I ask is that you keep out of the delegates' way. I'll pop in from time to time to check you are where you should be. I've arranged for you both to take your meals in my room too. Is that fine by you?'

'Of course. I'll make myself scarce.'

'Thank you, dear. Don't hesitate to let me know if there's anything you need. You'll find spare kit in the changing rooms.'

'Thanks.'

Darcie bolted her cereal down and went straight up to the housekeeper's room, reasoning that the sooner she got through her tasks, the quicker she could be out of Hugo's company and in the pool. To her dismay, he had beaten her there. He looked up when she came in, smiled to himself, then returned to his work, as though he had thought it some kind of race and considered himself the winner. Darcie slid into a seat at the far end of the table and pulled the pile of books towards her. Mrs Smith had left a note.

This was the best I could come up with at short notice – not exactly standard curriculum, but you might find them interesting. Please read and write a summary of one of the books by my return. GS.

Darcie leafed through the books – most were manuals on spying, with chapters on subjects like surveillance techniques, computer hacking and use of covert weapons. She shoved those ones aside; she didn't want to be sucked in to that world further than she already was. The last book was a history of espionage, starting with the Tudor court and leading to the present day. It at least felt more normal, closer to the kind of stuff she might have been doing in her history class right now had she not had to jump out the window. Darcie pushed her chair back, put her feet up on the table, and began to read.

At first it was distracting being in the same room as Hugo. She could hear him labouring over his essay, flipping the pages of a book on small arms and light weapons with an irritable snap. If anyone had asked her a few weeks back what she would be doing now, this would have been the last scenario she would have come up with. Finally, the diabolical goings-on in Elizabeth I's court snagged her attention and pulled her into her book.

'Who was that boy last night?' The suddenness of Hugo's question took her by surprise.

'Just a friend,' said Darcie, keeping her eyes on the page.

'How much does he know about you?'

So he was worried how much she'd said about him. He didn't trust her.

'Know what about me, exactly?'

'About you being a spy.'

'I'm not a spy.' Darcie put her feet on the floor

and bent over the paper, scratching out a title with the pen on the blank sheet.

'According to Mrs Smith, you are – a very good one. That's why they've started this scheme to train younger recruits.' Hugo yawned and stretched his arms, bored of being confined inside.

'I'm not a spy,' Darcie repeated.

'So what've you been doing over the last few months then? Mrs Smith said you'd just finished a mission.'

'Hugo, I really don't want to talk to you.'

'Fine. That's what all spies say.' He was smiling to himself again. He always had been a smug bighead. 'You know something, Darcie, I'm looking forward to training with you. The SNEs will be much more fun with you around.'

Darcie couldn't help asking, despite her intention to end all conversation. 'SNE? What's that?'

'Solo night-time expeditions. A walk in the park for you with your experience.'

'Shut up, Hugo.'

'Don't get me wrong – it was really cool how you got out of the car that night in Kenya and still managed to make it to the Country Club. I always wanted to know how you did it.'

She kicked herself for starting a normal conversation with him and making that truce last night: give him an inch and he'd take a mile – no, ten miles. 'Well, keep wondering.'

'I'll do you a deal –'

'Another deal?'

'Yeah, why not? If I beat you on one of the SNEs, you tell me how you did it.'

'No.'

'Why not?'

'Hugo, don't you have any idea what I feel about that – and about you? You'd be the last person I'd tell. I'm not playing your sick games.' Darcie could see that he was enjoying winding her up but she couldn't stop herself rising to the bait.

'Yeah, that's one thing I'm really sorry about. I know you had a huge crush on me in the spring and I disappointed you.' Hugo rocked back on his chair. 'Never did get that kiss, did you? Still, who knows? Not much competition for you here. I might get round to it.'

'Just shut up!' Darcie threw her book at him, catching him on the chest. The book collapsed to the floor, pages open, like an injured butterfly, wings bent.

'I was only joking!' Hugo protested, his manner

unconvincingly apologetic. 'Where's your sense of humour?'

'But it's not funny!' The urge to thump him was overwhelming. If she didn't get out of here, she couldn't be answerable for what would happen.

'Isn't it? I hate you – you hate me – and we get stuck together by the secretary general of the United Nations. I heard she was good at reconciling sworn enemies but this is taking it too far.'

Darcie swore at him.

'Tut, tut – I'll tell Carmen.'

Not caring if she got into trouble for leaving the room, Darcie stormed out, slamming the door behind her – and walked straight into the arrival of the delegations.

She ducked behind a suit of armour in a dark corner of the landing. Carmen was showing a party of grim- faced men up the stairs.

'General Paschuk, we've put you in the Nightingale Suite. It's lovely – very prettily decorated and calming,' the secretary general was saying brightly. 'Your staff are in the rooms on the same corridor, as you requested.'

A tall man with a shaven head towered over Carmen – it was impossible to know if he understood what she was saying: his face was set in a frown. He looked like a wrestler – his nose had clearly been broken on several occasions and he was missing two fingers on his left hand. He had the erect bearing of one who had spent many hours on the parade ground. Darcie felt sure it would take more than a stay in the Nightingale Suite to sweeten his disposition.

Carmen seemed relieved when she was able to turn away to his colleague. 'Deputy Mila?'

A woman with dyed red hair and a drab, brown business suit stepped forward. She was wearing puce sandals, her stocking-covered toes flexing, betraying her nervousness among all this splendour.

'I've put you next to me down here – not as grand as this wing but I think it's more homely. Would you like to follow me?'

'Thank you, Secretary General,' the Tazbek woman replied in a heavily accented voice. She played with a box of cigarettes, obviously desperate to light up but too cowed by her surroundings to risk it.

The secretary general touched her lightly on the arm, a soothing pat. 'No, no, call me Carmen. The formalities are yet to begin. I've made sure you have a balcony in case you need to smoke.'

Deputy Mila gave the secretary general a relieved

smile and followed her in the direction of the guest rooms.

Darcie waited for the crowd to flow by before coming out from her hiding place. The upper corridors were going to be very busy for the next few hours so she decided that the best place for her to keep out the way would be down at the pool. A hundred lengths should wash away the nauseating feeling left by Hugo Kraus.

The pool was deserted when she arrived: its surface eerily smooth and glassy in the dim lighting. Darcie rifled through a pile of swimming costumes until she found one that would more or less fit. She undressed quickly, leaving her clothes in a neat pile in the empty changing room. Pausing at the edge of the water, she wriggled her toes on the brink, took a breath and dived in, shattering the stillness into thousands of ripples. Darcie completed the first length underwater; tumble turned and came up for a breath. The water made her feel clean and washed away the frustration of sharing the same space as Hugo. It was only a small pool, so a hundred lengths was no real challenge. She decided to push herself to two hundred. Concentrating only on her strokes, she began her marathon.

When she reached a hundred and twenty-five,

two people entered the pool area. Glancing to the side as she took a breath, she made out the baldhead of the general she had seen on the stairs and one of his aides. She hoped they were not going to join her in the pool and spoil her peace. Maybe they were going to the gym – military types probably would want to keep fit. But they stayed where they were. The general watched her for a moment then turned away to speak to the man at his side, chopping at the air as he explained something. He pointed at each door into the basement sports centre then stabbed at a map the aide was holding. By the time Darcie had turned at the far end of the pool, they were gone.

It was probably nothing – just finding their way around, Darcie told herself. But try as she might to regain her previous state of calm, she couldn't get the two men out of her head. Having recently spent time with the SAS, she knew a recce when she saw one. Why would the Tazbeks want to do that?

Having completed her lengths, Darcie climbed out and showered. Her body was zinging with energy after the exercise. The swim had also set her mind on a different track – it was a relief to be pondering the behaviour of people for whom she had no responsibility, no contact even, rather than obsess about Hugo.

As the prospect of returning to the housekeeper's room with its resident pain-in-the-behind was not enticing, Darcie escaped into the fresh air. Delegates were gathered in the library for morning coffee. She gave them a wide berth and headed for the coastal path. A policeman on patrol with an Alsatian nodded a greeting, otherwise she seemed to have the grounds to herself. Rather than go down to the cove again, she decided to explore the promontory beyond the house. The path wound up on to higher ground, giving her a good view down on St Helen's which was built on a kind of ledge or notch in the hillside, providing some shelter in this exposed spot. She noticed a long, low building hugging the western wall – Gladys had mentioned that there was a rifle range and she guessed that must be it. She reached the cliff edge and lay flat on her stomach in the grass to look over. Waves broke white on the rocks below. A tiny beach, inaccessible to man, nestled at the foot of the cliff, a grey seal basking in the sunshine, unsuspecting of any onlooker. Darcie watched with delight as the creature flopped lazily on its back, waving a flipper languidly in the air.

She was so absorbed by the view that she didn't hear the men approaching until they started speaking not ten metres away. They hadn't spotted her as she was hidden in the undergrowth. Harsh voices, speaking in Russian. Darcie cautiously swivelled round. The general's aide was talking to a man she'd not seen before, though he had the same look of a hardened fighter and a big walrus moustache that would have been funny if he hadn't been so scary. They both had binoculars and were standing with their backs to her surveying St Helen's, very much as she had done only a few minutes before.

Why were they not in the conference? That was why they were here after all – to make peace around a table; this was no time for a country walk.

The grass began to prickle her bare arms but something told her it was best not to be seen. She lay very still, waiting for them to move on, as they eventually did some five minutes later.

Something was going on in the Tazbek delegation: that much was clear. Darcie lay on her back looking at the grey clouds overhead, considering what she should do. But what had she really seen? A few men talking and looking at maps? Not much to make a fuss about. Still . . .

She pulled out her mobile and pondered whom to ring. She was under strict orders only to talk to her dad on a secure line as he was at another of SIS's secret locations; the only safe phone she could use was in Gladys's room. That left Stingo. He'd asked her not to call. But then, when had she ever done what she was told?

'Are you stalking me or something?' Stingo asked as soon as she dialled his number.

'Yeah, I'm your worst nightmare, I know, I know.'

'Is it Hugo?'

'No. He's exactly what you'd expect – full of himself.'

'So what's up?'

The line crackled. Darcie stood up, trying to find a stronger signal. 'I'm not sure. Just a hunch.'

'Better make this quick, Darcie, we're really not supposed to be talking to each other – that wasn't just a story I made up to rid myself of an annoying teenager.'

'It's the Tazbeks – they're acting funny.'

'Based on what – your extensive knowledge of Tazbek culture?' Stingo couldn't resist mocking.

'No, based on spending more time than's good for me with you lot. They're going over this place like they're planning something.'

'What've you seen?' Stingo sounded interested at last.

'The general and his aide were checking out the basement – entrances and exits – and I've just seen two of them doing the same for the outside. They've got binoculars and maps – it's not a casual thing.'

Stingo was silent for a moment. 'They might just be looking after their own security. According to the Russians, Paschuk is a terrorist: they're probably afraid of being double-crossed by our government and handed over to the Russian authorities.'

'Are they right to worry? Is the government going to do that?'

'I dunno, Darcie, I'm only a soldier, remember, but I doubt it very much – not with Carmen Lopez there. But I don't blame them for being cautious – men like that wouldn't still be alive if they hadn't learnt to watch their backs long ago.'

'Yeah, you're right, that's probably it.' Darcie was half-convinced by this explanation. 'So you think I shouldn't say anything?'

'Go with your gut. What do you want to do?'

Darcie laughed. 'Well, that's easy: I want to get out of here and go somewhere normal – watch a film while eating popcorn, go to sleep in my own bed.'

'I know. I'm grounded too at the moment. They're keeping me on base while they investigate the allegations about us. It'd take something big to get me out of here. But you know what I meant. Do you know any of the security guys there? You could draw their attention to what you've seen.'

Darcie shivered: it was beginning to spit with rain. 'No, I don't know them – Hugo's working with them though. I s'pose I could ask him to mention it.'

Stingo gave a snort of disgust. 'Best not to ask him to do anything for you.'

'Yeah, you're right. There are only two other people I know here: one is the housekeeper, who's probably more interested in the fact that I bunked off all morning, and Carmen Lopez, but I'm the last person she's got a minute for right now.'

'Yeah, world peace is so time consuming.' Darcie could hear voices at Stingo's end of the conversation. 'Look, I've gotta go.' He sounded worried. 'Keep in touch.'

And he ended the call.

Darcie stood undecided with the phone still in her hand. The rain was now falling in sheets, mixed with salty spray whipped off the waves breaking on the rocks below. Her T-shirt was soaked and her hair straggling down her neck. Stingo's judgement had never failed her: if he thought she should act on her gut feeling, however silly that made her look, then she should do so. Slipping the phone into her pocket, she jogged back to the house, ducked in through the main entrance, and bolted upstairs to her own room, hoping no one had seen. She'd had a new idea: if she could get to Gladys's room, she could call her dad – he was bound to know what to do. No harm in trying for a second opinion.

She slipped silently down the stairs to the

corridor below, not having a clear idea of exactly where the room was but guessing it was more or less just below hers from what Gladys had said yesterday. She found an unmarked door right at the end that looked promising, hesitated, then tried the handle.

'Oh, excuse me.' She'd found the right room but had forgotten Gladys had told her it would be needed for the conference. The new occupiers were none other than Carmen Lopez and John Riddell, the foreign secretary, deep in conversation.

Carmen looked up and smiled when she saw who it was. 'Ah, Darcie, how's your day so far?'

'Fine, thank you, ma'am.'

'Did you want something?'

Riddell had barely registered her presence, continuing to shuffle the papers in front of him, frowning.

'No, no, I'm sorry to interrupt.' She made to close the door.

'John, have you met Darcie?' Carmen said, getting to her feet and stretching by the window. She seemed quite pleased to be interrupted. 'She lives here.'

Riddell looked up at the girl in the doorway for the first time. 'Darcie? Darcie Lock by any chance?'

'Yes, sir.' Darcie shuffled her feet awkwardly.

Riddell smiled and got up to shake her hand, then converted the gesture to a pat on the shoulder. 'I'm delighted to meet you. I've heard a lot about you from your grandfather among others. Very impressive.'

Carmen's ears pricked up. 'Oh? Is my Darcie famous already?'

'In certain circles. You must have a reason for coming in here, Darcie. Did you want to speak to one of us?'

Darcie shook her head. 'Er, no, I just wanted to talk to my dad on the secure line.' She guessed he would know about her father and would understand.

'We're going back into session in about ten minutes: why don't you come back then?' Riddell suggested. He took out a pack of chewing gum and opened a strip with a sigh. 'Trying to give up smok-ing,' he explained, seeing that she was watching. 'Would offer you some but it's some foul nicotine replacement stuff. I've chosen a bad time to break the habit: this conference is enough to crack anyone's will power.'

This admission made him less daunting, more human. Darcie hesitated: fate could not have handed her a better moment to convey her suspicions to those who should hear them. 'Actually, there is something I wanted to mention – I wasn't sure if it was anything to worry about – I mean, I might just be imagining things . . .'

Riddell beckoned her into the room. 'With your record, I doubt that very much. Take a seat.'

She perched on the edge of a chair, sensing the genuine welcome in the room. The two politicians were on easy terms with each other, making a natural team, but she couldn't quite believe she was in conversation with the British foreign secretary and the secretary general of the United Nations – bizarre!

'So, what's up?' Riddell gave her his full attention.

'The Tazbeks are acting strangely. I've bumped into them all over the place this morning with maps and binoculars. They might just be being careful, but it seemed kind of funny to me when you've provided security for the conference.'

Riddell scratched his chin, glanced at Carmen, who was studiously keeping her own counsel, then he pressed an intercom on the table. 'James, can you come in here a moment, please?'

The door opened and Riddell's private secretary entered, his auburn hair caught back in a neat stubby pigtail. He caught sight of Darcie and immediately began to apologize.

'I'm so sorry, sir.' He took Darcie's elbow to pull her up. 'I don't know how it happened. I'll make sure she's sent away.'

The foreign secretary screwed the gum wrapper into a ball and threw it at James. 'Sit down, you idiot. Darcie is here at our invitation.'

'Oh.' James changed direction with admirable skill. He let go of her arm and held out his hand. 'I'm sorry – I got the wrong end of the stick. James Harlem.'

'Darcie Lock.' She shook his hand, warming to a man who didn't flinch at being called an idiot by his boss and bombarded with paper darts.

James's smile broadened on hearing her name. 'Ah, that Darcie! Now I understand.'

Seeing his reaction, Carmen could not bear to be kept in the dark any longer. 'What is it about this girl, John?' she asked in a wheedling tone.

Riddell gave a teasing, enigmatic smile. 'I couldn't possibly say, Carmen. Darcie's one of HMG's best kept secrets. You really don't want to know.'

Darcie blushed and looked down at her scuffed trainers.

James deftly covered the awkward pause that followed this remark. 'You wanted me, sir?'

'Yes. Darcie's been around and about this morning and noticed the Tazbeks looking the place over with rather too keen an interest. Can you give the security people a heads-up on this?'

'Yes, sir. Though I really don't think there's much to worry about. All luggage was discreetly but thoroughly searched – everyone came in empty-handed, unless you count the large number of vodka bottles in Mr Turgenov's suitcase. The only oddity was the extra men on Paschuk's team, but we gather that is because he'd fallen out with his colleagues and wants his own people around him to even up the numbers. We could hardly object as there's plenty of room for them all. We have a tight security cordon around the site – no one's coming in by land, sea or air without us knowing it first.' James gave Darcie a reassuring nod. 'But I'll keep an eye on things, don't worry.'

Carmen leaned forward and stroked Darcie's cheek, her dark eyes searching the girl's face for some clue. 'Well, you are a mystery, my little friend. Forgive me for asking but are you all right? You look a little stressed.'

'Just a bit. Hugo and I don't get on,' Darcie admitted, giving Carmen a rueful smile and moving back from the caress, embarrassed by the gesture.

'What a shame – and such a handsome young man too.'

Darcie made a face. Carmen laughed.

'What? There's another of you around the place, is there?' asked Riddell.

'Not another of me,' Darcie corrected. 'There's a boy staying here – he's on a training programme.'

'Exactly – another one. Well, keep your eyes peeled, both of you.' He glanced at his watch. 'We'd better get back to the bear pit.'

Carmen stood up. 'Yes. It's time. See you later, Darcie. I'm sorry we can't invite you to the banquet this evening but if you want to see the razzle-dazzle, you could always sneak on to the minstrels' gallery.'

'Thanks. I might do that.'

Feeling more at peace now she had delivered her message, Darcie wandered back to the housekeeper's room. Hugo was still hard at work, crouched over his laptop.

'Mrs Jefferson wants to see you,' he said gruffly. 'Where've you been?'

She toyed with saying 'none of your business' but then took a different tack. 'Talking to John Riddell and Carmen Lopez.'

He grunted sceptically. 'Yeah, and I've been deep

in conversation with Santa Claus and the Tooth Fairy.'

'Mr Riddell wants us both to keep an eye on the Tazbeks.'

'Are you serious?' Hugo stopped typing and sat back to stare at her.

'Yeah, your first mission.' Darcie enjoyed his astonishment. 'I tipped them off that the Tazbeks are up to something and Mr Riddell agreed. What exactly, we don't know.'

Excitement flared in Hugo's pale blue eyes. 'What are our orders?'

Darcie smiled at his super-serious expression. 'Stand down, soldier. He doesn't want us to do anything in particular, just use our highly trained instincts to see what's happening around the house.'

Hugo missed her mocking tone. 'Right, I'll take the grounds – you do the inside.'

Darcie began to laugh. 'You're priceless, Hugo! There's a whole police protection team in the area – don't you think they've got that covered? If you start messing around out there, you'll end up getting shot as an intruder.'

'So you're winding me up? There's no mission?' Hugo frowned.

Darcie decided she really had to put him out of

his misery. 'Not exactly. All Mr Riddell asked us to do was to be alert. As we don't officially exist, we can hang around, seeing things others wouldn't. Nothing more.'

Hugo was still annoyed at her for teasing him. 'You're not taking this seriously, are you?' He pressed a few keys on his computer and a closely spaced essay running to many pages began to spew from the printer.

'You're wrong.' Darcie picked up her book again. 'I just don't take myself as seriously as you do.'

Hugo stapled his work together, giving no sign that he'd registered her remark. He put it in the in-tray on the desk. 'Right, that's finished. I'm off to practise on the range. Enjoy.' He nodded at her pile of books and left with a smug look on his face.

Feeling the atmosphere had improved vastly now he'd gone, Darcie settled down to work. Apart from the arrival of a sandwich lunch, nothing of note happened over the next few hours. Bored of the history of espionage, Darcie turned on the house-keeper's television only to see distant views of St Helen's being broadcast on the lunchtime news. The reporter, standing in a chill wind from the look of her pinched face, was burbling on about how the talks were being held away from the press.

'So what you're really saying,' Darcie said aloud to the screen, 'is that you have no news.'

She switched off. Making world peace was more boring than she expected.

Down in the conference room, there was indeed little to report. The Russian delegation, led by the not totally sober Mr Turgenov, Russian Minister of the Interior, were sticking by their position: Tazbekistan was part of Russia. Independence was not possible. Turgenov, a big white-haired bear of a man, along with the other four Russians at the table, chain-smoked and drank like fish, but his thoughts were not the least befuddled on this issue.

Carmen took some comfort in the fact that Deputy Rosa Mila, the unofficial president of the breakaway republic, seemed ready to meet the Russians halfway. Despite Mila's unfortunate fashion sense her mind was faultlessly turned out, it seemed.

'We want to run our own affairs, police ourselves, but we are happy to accept Russia's lead in foreign relations and defence,' Deputy Mila offered.

Most of the Tazbeks nodded their agreement to these remarks, all except the shaven-headed General Paschuk, who sat like a brooding hawk at the far end of the table. When Carmen tried to include him in discussions, asking for his opinion, he gave a curt reply. 'Deputy Mila knows what I think.' He would not be drawn further.

By the end of the day, Carmen felt exhausted by the fruitless exchanges. She made the best of things by summing up their respective positions and declaring the meeting closed until the morning – 'After we have had the opportunity to get to know each other and build trust at tonight's banquet.'

Carmen had decided to dress up for the banquet to add, as she had told Darcie earlier, a little razzle-dazzle to the proceedings. Alone in her room, she smiled at her reflection: men might have to stick by the dull colours of the lounge suit or dinner jacket, but she could indulge in a hot red number from the house of Tsui, her favourite Hong Kong designer. Such a shame the designer had fallen into disgrace. The dress hugged her trim figure and fell smoothly to the floor, hem higher at the front, a train at the back, reminiscent of a flamenco dancer. Well, she would certainly need to be quick on her toes tonight to negotiate the diplomatic dance that these events required.

Somehow, she would have to avoid the subject of the numerous human rights abuses inflicted by both sides, the mounting toll of fatalities, the widows and orphans, and 'ethnically cleansed' villages. Tonight she would have to ignore the fact that General Paschuk was a beast and Turgenov a drunken fool, both unable to show the true statesmanship required to salvage this conference. At least John Riddell was on her side – it was good to feel there was an ally in the room. The Brit was another free spirit like her.

Applying gloss to her lipstick, Carmen surveyed the end result. She had deliberately cultivated the image of herself as a fiery South American woman, finding it disarmed the more cold-blooded men who ruled most of the world. She liked and admired Rosa Mila, the economist who found herself nominated as head of Tazbekistan, but the real power lay with the men of iron behind her. They were Carmen's target tonight, the key to breaking out of the current dead-lock in the talks. She blew a kiss at her reflection and gave an ironic smile: watch out, General Paschuk, the UN was about to launch its biggest ever charm offensive.

Up on the balcony, Darcie looked down on the heads of the crowd below. Carmen wandered from group to group, a dash of red in the sombre colours, moving like a humming bird going from flower to flower. Darcie had been amazed at the stunning entrance a few minutes before as Carmen paused in the double doorway to allow everyone to admire her outfit. John Riddell had looked dumb-struck as she had glided up to him and cheekily flounced her skirts like a dancer preparing to perform. He was not the only one – nearly all the men in the room were following her with their eyes.

Nearly all.

Darcie could not fail to notice that General Paschuk, dressed in a chilling black uniform with gold trimmings, had barely spared the UN secretary general a glance. His thoughts were fixed on his untouched glass of champagne, paying no attention to James Harlem who was valiantly trying to engage him in conversation. Interpreters hovered at the arm of all the major players in the negotiations; General Paschuk's might as well have gone home and put her feet up for all the use that was being made of her services.

Poor Deputy Mila had turned up in another wardrobe disaster: a pink floaty number that clashed horribly with her red hair. That didn't dampen her spirits as she swigged her cocktail. Darcie was beginning to feel a fondness for the woman who could commit such fashion crimes and not care.

A gong sounded in the hall and the guests made their way to their places at the banquet table. Waiters glided in from a side door with silver soup tureens balanced on their arms; Darcie saw with a jolt of surprise that Jake was among them, scarcely recognizable in his white uniform. He hadn't told her he did silver service, but it made sense: she supposed that was how he funded his vast music collection. She wished he'd look up and spot her, somehow let her know that everything was going to be all right between them. If he would only trust her, listen to her side of the story; but then, what could she say?

He disappeared back into the kitchen. Behind the scenes, Kito and Aunt Josephine would be frantically lining up each dish of the complicated meal. Darcie had grabbed a menu on her way up here and knew there were five courses – a nightmare for the staff. Not much fun for those at the table either, she mused, watching Carmen try and make conversation with the miserable General Paschuk while the Russian minister, Turgenov, leered at her drunkenly on the other side. Darcie looked at her watch: eight o'clock. She'd seen enough.

On the point of leaving, Darcie heard someone strike a fork against a glass with a ringing sound. Thinking that perhaps Carmen was about to make a speech, she peered over the edge and saw that General Paschuk was on his feet. Deputy Mila froze, her drink halfway to her lips. A confused babble died away – this was unscripted but all were determined to be polite and give the taciturn man their attention. The interpreter stood up but the general waved her away.

'Ladies and gentleman,' he began in surprisingly good English, 'I have an announcement.'

The doors opened and three of the general's men entered, guns levelled at the guests. Darcie muffled her cry of surprise; Carmen gripped the stem of her wine glass, knuckles white.

'There has been a change of plan. As I speak, my forces in Tazbekistan have declared a state of emergency and a military government has taken over from our inadequate leader, Deputy Mila.' He nodded ironically to the ashen woman two seats away. Gently, John Riddell placed his hand on Rosa Mila's shaking wrist, a sign of solidarity with his Tazbek guest. 'I have been named as head of state.'

'This is an outrage!' spluttered Minster Turgenov, surging to his feet. Despite swigging back the pre-dinner drinks, he sobered up with lightning speed.

Paschuk gave him an icy smile. 'Sit down or I'll shoot you,' he said in Russian, drawing a pistol from his pocket and levelling it at the minister. Turgenov collapsed into his seat, fury etched in the clenched lines around his mouth, his white hair hanging lopsided over one brow.

'As I was saying,' continued Paschuk in English once again, 'I am now in charge. My men have taken control of this building and I now demand that our British host,' he nodded at Riddell, 'order his external security patrol to withdraw to a minimum of one kilometre from the house. Failure to do so will result in the death of a number of people in this room, starting with our Russian friend Mr Turgenov here. Do you agree?'

Riddell rose to his feet, his hands trembling. 'General Paschuk, this is madness –'

Paschuk firmly pressed the gun against Turgenov's temple, posture rigid. 'Do you agree?'

Riddell lowered his head, clenching his fists. Faced with such an ultimatum, he had no choice. 'I'll give the order.'

'Good.'

The side door opened and an armed man ushered

the kitchen staff into the room. Darcie could see Kito still clutching his ladle, Jake looking bewildered by his side. Through the main doors straggled a confused line of secretaries, the technicians, communications staff and finally the housekeeper – all prodded along by two more of Paschuk's men. At gunpoint, the hostages were made to sit along one wall. Icy fear gripped Darcie seeing Jake with weapons trained on him.

'Is that everyone?' asked the general. His aide consulted a list, the same one as had been at reception when Darcie had checked Hugo's room.

'*Da.*'

'How many dead?' He kept to English, wanting his audience to understand the answer.

'One – a policeman. He got in the way.'

'The other protection officers?'

'In the basement.'

Paschuk received the news with cool approval. 'Excellent. Now, I think it is time we restarted negotiations.' He turned to address Carmen and Turgenov. 'My first demand is that the Russian troops occupying Tazbekistan stay in their barracks while the handover of power to me takes place. From this moment on, for every casualty of a Russian bullet in my country, I will take a life here.'

Darcie began to back away to the door out of the gallery, crawling on her hands and knees. This couldn't be happening. It was supposed to be safe here, a peace conference for heaven's sake! Where had all the guns come from? According to James Harlem, the luggage had been checked; no one should have been able to bring weapons in with them. They must have been here already.

The firing range. She'd not taken much notice when Hugo had declared his intention to go target shooting but that of course meant that the weapons had been here all the time, under lock and key admittedly, but accessible to a determined assault. And if Hugo had been in the range this afternoon, did that mean he had been there when the Tazbeks had broken in? One person was dead. Had it been Hugo who got in the way?

Darcie had thought she would not worry about Hugo but that was before his death became a real possibility. Bully that he was, it was still sickening to think he may have died in terror, riddled with bullets. She wouldn't wish that on her worst enemy. But if she was right, she was the only person on the loose in the building.

Think, she urged herself, trying not to panic. What to do first? Try and contact someone, obviously, so that meant fetching her phone – and that meant going back to her room where she had left it to recharge.

Running lightly up the stairs, praying the Tazbeks were too busy herding everyone into the hall to be on the prowl, she reached her bedroom without being seen. She ducked inside and dived for the phone, yanking the charger from the wall. They didn't know about her – and it had to stay that way. She quickly removed all traces of her presence – helped by the fact that she had no luggage. Straightening the towels in the bathroom, smoothing the bed, she quickly made the room look as if it hadn't been occupied lately. Now she needed a safe place to make her call.

Darcie put her ear to the door. She could hear voices in the distance – it had to be the Tazbeks searching the house for anyone they'd missed on their initial sweep. Paschuk's military mind was leaving nothing to chance. She couldn't risk the main stairs again and she had to get out of here. If she couldn't go down, then the only option was up. Remembering what she had seen from the outside, she knew that this part of the building had a pitched roof. There had to be an attic above. Quickly searching for a way in, she found a service hatch outside Hugo's room. She pushed the trapdoor open with a broom from the cleaner's closet, climbed on a chair she had balanced precariously on a small table, and pulled herself up. That left two telltale pieces of furniture in the middle of the corridor. Darcie hooked the chair with the end of the broom and lifted it up through the hatch.

The voices were getting nearer.

'Keep calm; concentrate,' she urged herself. Would they notice the table? Probably. Leaning out as far as she could without falling, she used the broom to push the table back against the wall. She managed it in a fashion – it wasn't straight but at least it was no longer so obvious. She closed the trapdoor and lay with her ear pressed against it.

Booted feet marched down the corridor, kicking open each door. Intermittently, a voice would shout in Russian – Darcie guessed it was something along the lines of 'all clear'. Now they were below her. The door to Hugo's room was forced open. Voices. She held her breath. Then they went on their way.

Darcie waited until she was sure no one was around and turned on her phone. It rang immediately.

'Darcie, are you all right? What's happening in

there?' It was Stingo. 'I'm watching the news – there's panic. No one knows what's going on.'

'Oh, Stingo, thank God it's you. I don't know what to do. General Paschuk has taken everyone hostage – he's holding them in the dining hall. Some are in the basement – the protection team I think. I don't know how many men he's got – I've seen at least four.'

Stingo swore. 'But you, you're OK?'

'Yes, I'm well hidden for the moment. Look, can you get a message to Dad for me?'

'Leave it with me. Stay out of sight. We'll get you out of there.'

[8]

Westminster, London: stormy, 15°C

In the crisis meeting room in the basement of Downing Street, the emergency session got hastily underway. Senior ministers, police chiefs and intelligence officers took their places around the prime minister. Everyone was reeling from the disastrous turn of events at St Helen's.

'How the hell could it happen?' the prime minister barked to the head of the diplomatic protection squad.

The hapless man shook his head. 'No idea, sir.

No one took any weapons into St Helen's – we made sure of that.'

'But they must have guns now – I can't imagine our men allowing them to take over without an over-whelming show of force,' added the head of MI5, Gerald Fosdyke.

Christopher Lock slid into his chair. 'Well, Gerry, you can prepare for most things, but not the attack from the inside. I imagine they raided the firing range.'

'You've a firing range there?' spluttered the prime minister, leafing through his brief. 'I had no idea.'

'Yes, sir. St Helen's is a training college for my operatives. We did not foresee when we set it up that it might be taken over by a band of terrorists invited in through the front door.'

The prime minister did not miss Christopher's reproving tone. 'Well, how on earth were we to know that they were planning a stunt like this?'

Christopher Lock refrained from mentioning his conversation warning John Riddell that something might go wrong. It was unproductive during a crisis to say 'I told you so'.

'So what are we going to do?' interrupted the minister of defence, a stout man with a florid complexion. He wiped his brow with a handkerchief.

'How many inside?' asked the prime minister.

'One hundred and forty-two civilians, including our minister and the secretary general. At least ten terrorists,' supplied Gerald Fosdyke.

'Options?'

'Negotiate or send in the SAS.'

'Recommendation?'

Fosdyke tugged at his collar. 'It's hard to say without better intelligence. We don't know how serious Paschuk is about killing the hostages.'

'If even one Russian delegate gets harmed – or, God forbid, the secretary general – then there will be hell to pay in the international community,' warned the prime minister. 'We can't afford to get this wrong after the balls-up on security.'

'But, sir, we are playing this blind – we've no idea what's happening in there. It's one of the most protected buildings in the country so we can't even eavesdrop. We've no one inside.'

Christopher Lock waited a beat to break his news. 'Perhaps my department can be of assistance. We do in fact still have two people in the building and I know for a fact that one of them is not being held by the Tazbeks.'

'What! Why didn't you say before?' exclaimed the prime minister.

Christopher ignored this remark. 'I have one of my men on the phone to the agent even as we speak.' By which he meant that Michael Lock was currently in contact with his terrified daughter.

'What's your operative like? Can we trust him to gather the information for us without getting caught? General Paschuk's demanded no interference from outside. I wouldn't like to give him the excuse to start shooting.'

'My agent is very discreet. No one will suspect her of anything,' and Christopher, convinced that his granddaughter's age would protect her even if she was apprehended – though, he hoped, of course, that it wouldn't come to that.

'Good. Order her to assess how serious the Tazbeks are in carrying out their threats.' The prime minister turned quickly to another of his ministers. 'What's the Russian position on all this?'

The minister shook his head. 'The Russians won't allow themselves to bow to hostage threats so there's no hope of them showing restraint in the Tazbek capital, Jalabad, let alone keep their troops in barracks throughout the rest of Tazbekistan. General Paschuk's men have a fight on their hands back home.'

'So we can expect casualties?'

'Yes.'

'Then I fear we'll find out sooner than we would like just how desperate Paschuk is. Get the SAS in theatre and stand by. We'll wait for your operative's assessment, Christopher, and take a final decision then.'

Michael strongly resisted the attempt to make use of his daughter until Gladys pointed out that Darcie's best hope of rescue lay in a well-briefed mission. It would do her no good if the SAS stormed in and fumbled the operation because they misjudged what was going on. Darcie might be able to provide the information needed to negotiate a peaceful end to the siege.

Michael called his daughter again. 'Are you all right, darling?'

'Yes, Dad. Still here.' Darcie was shivering as she crouched in a corner of the attic, wondering if it was feasible just to hide up here until things were sorted out below. But what about Jake, Carmen and all the others downstairs? Could she sit here while that madman picked them off one by one? Someone had to rescue them. 'What's been decided your end?'

'We need to know if Paschuk is serious about his

threat to start killing the hostages.' Michael tried to keep his voice steady. 'And we want to discover where his men are deployed. Can you find out what's happening for us?'

'Me?' Darcie's voice squeaked. 'You want me to go down there again?'

'Only if you can do it without getting caught. Can you?'

'I don't know – I s'pose I won't know until I try, will I?'

'We need to find out because either we negotiate an end to this or bust you all out. The first is the better option – the second is bound to have . . . casualties.'

Darcie searched for the courage she would need to make herself emerge from her hiding place. 'OK, Dad. I'll give it a go. I'll have to turn my phone off but I'll call as soon as I'm somewhere safe.'

'All right, darling.' There was a catch in her father's voice. 'Don't take any unnecessary risks – if you think you're going to be seen, call it off. I mean it. OK?'

'OK.'

'I love you.'

'Love you too.' Darcie switched off the phone, took a deep breath and dropped through the trapdoor. She landed lightly on her feet. All clear. Treading softly, she made her way back downstairs, heading for the minstrels' gallery. She tried not to think what scene might greet her when she did look down into the dining hall. Jake would be so scared. She prayed Paschuk had not turned his attention on any of the staff. With that worrying thought, she crept on to the balcony and peeked through the banisters. The hostages were now in two groups: women on one side, men on the other. Carmen was sitting with her arm around Josephine; Jake was back to back with his dad, hands tied together. The Tazbeks appeared to have bound the men, but left the women free – some kind of misplaced chivalry. Deputy Mila surprised Darcie: the woman who had looked so timid was arguing furiously with the general, waving her arms in the air. John Riddell was tied to the Russian minister – both looked grim as a man stood over them with an assault rifle.

Tired of her tirade, General Paschuk pushed Rosa Mila aside and walked over to Carmen.

'Secretary General?'

Carmen lifted her chin but didn't get up. 'General Paschuk.'

'I want you to speak to the negotiators and tell them that my patience is almost exhausted. I want a public pledge from the Russians that they will agree to my demands. It must be announced by the president on television so there is no chance of them backing down from their promise later.'

'I will ask, but you and I both know you won't get your way.'

Paschuk frowned. 'Then I will kill a hostage at dawn. And another an hour later – one every hour until they do as I say.'

Darcie decided she'd heard enough. She crept out into the corridor on the alert for any patrols. There had only been four armed men in the room which meant at least six were somewhere in the house and grounds. She ran up the stairs to the top floor, planning to go back to her hiding place. Just as she turned into her corridor, she felt someone yank her from behind and pull her into the cleaner's cupboard. A large hand stifled her cry.

'Shh!' It was Hugo. 'The patrol's up here.'

Darcie stood squeezed up against Hugo, ears straining to hear what was going on outside. Footsteps approached, then paused outside the cupboard. A lighter clicked and cigarette smoke drifted in through the chinks under the door. The patrol was obviously relaxed enough to take a break for a smoke, but did it have to be right outside the cupboard? Darcie became uncomfortably aware of how close she was to Hugo. His hand was still over her mouth as if he didn't trust her not to give them away. She dared not push it aside in case the men outside heard the scuffle. Long minutes passed, then the patrol resumed, footsteps disappearing into the distance.

Darcie pulled away from Hugo and stepped out of the cupboard, wiping her wrist across her mouth to dispel the taste left by his hand.

'You OK?' he whispered.

Darcie nodded. 'I've got to report in.'

'You're in contact with the outside? Good. The patrol won't be back for ten minutes – let's use my room.' Rather than waste time climbing up to the attic, Darcie followed him. They didn't dare turn on the light so had to fumble their way in the dark. The keypad of the mobile gave off a greenish glow as Darcie filed her report with her dad, adding that she'd met up with Hugo. 'What do you want us to do now?' she asked, hoping he'd order them to go back into hiding.

'Give me five minutes,' Michael said.

'OK, but quickly – the patrol is due around then.'

Hugo had spent the time changing into his camouflage gear. 'What're our orders?' he asked, discreetly checking the view of the courtyard. 'Two men down there – I could take them out if they want.'

Darcie realised then that Hugo was the last person she'd choose to have on her side during a hostage siege. 'You can't do that – it would tell the Tazbeks they've missed us and might make them start shooting. Someone's dead already.'

Hugo moved back from the window. 'I know – one of the policemen. He tried to stop them breaking into the armoury.'

'Where were you?'

'On the range. I hid behind the targets while they cleared out the guns. Didn't even leave me one.'

Darcie wasn't unhappy about that, knowing from experience that idiots with guns were a danger to everyone. And Hugo was definitely an idiot.

'Anyway, Hugo, Gladys will probably want us to lie low. The last thing they want is more hostages.'

He stared at her. 'Lie low? You'd be happy to go off and hide when all those people are down there with guns pointing at them?'

'I'm just being realistic.'

'You're being a coward.'

Despite it being Hugo making the criticism, she felt the insult. It was true: she was scared. 'So, hero, what do you think we should do?' she asked bitterly.

'I think the best plan is to try and free the men in the basement – move the odds in our favour. Even unarmed, numbers can count for a lot.'

'You'll get yourself killed if you try to pull a stunt like that.'

'Yeah, well, at least I'd've tried. If you have your way, we'll let that Paschuk nutter walk all over us.'

His tone needled her. 'Really? I'm surprised you feel like that. After all, he seems just your type – trying to take over his country – power crazy –'

Hugo picked a baseball bat out of the wardrobe. 'Oh yeah? Shows you how much you know about me, doesn't it, Darcie Lock? I wouldn't take a bunch of innocent people hostage.'

Darcie had had enough of his lecturing. 'You wouldn't, huh? So what about me? You didn't have any problem keeping me locked up when it was you and your crazy father with the guns! You hurt my friend – sent me off to be killed – had a go at me yourself, if I remember right. So don't pretend you're better than Paschuk, 'cause you're not!'

Hugo put his face right up to hers. 'You were no innocent bystander, remember – you came to spy on us.'

'So I asked for it, did I?'

'Your problem, Darcie, is you don't understand about power.'

'Your problem, Hugo, is you don't have a conscience.'

They held each other's eye for a moment until Hugo broke away. 'Fine. See how you manage on your own. I'm off to do something about this mess if you won't.'

'But orders –'

'I'm not waiting around for the patrol to find me. Tell them I'm off to break the siege.' Darcie tried to stop him but he was out of the door before she could reach him. The phone rang. Cursing, Darcie took the call.

'Dad, Hugo's gone AWOL.'

Michael swore. 'Can't you get him back?'

'I can try, but he's armed with a baseball bat and has some idea about freeing the men in the basement. He won't listen to me.'

'In that case, there's nothing you can do. He'll have to take his chances. We want you to go back and listen in on what's happening for as long as you can do so safely. Have they discovered the balcony yet?'

'Well, it's not exactly hidden, but they think

they've got everyone so they're not guarding it.'

'Good. We're planning to send in a team just before dawn when everyone is least alert but we need to know if the situation changes. Got that?'

'Yeah, I'll do my best.'

Back on the minstrels' gallery, Darcie found that little had changed in her absence. A television had been brought in and put on the top table; it had the twenty-four-hour news channel playing. Deprived of any closer view of St Helen's than could be had from the end of the drive, the reporter had augmented her coverage, adding interviews with the hostages' relatives. Darcie's attention was caught by Jake's mum, weeping before the cameras.

'My Kito, my boy, they're all in there!' she wept. 'My sister-in-law, my son's girlfriend – all of them.'

Darcie suddenly realised that Mrs Bridges was referring to her. She just hoped the Tazbeks weren't paying attention. The general was watching the television, brow furrowed, but he gave no sign he'd caught the significance of what was being said.

The relative calm in the hall was suddenly broken. Shots rang out from somewhere in the building. Darcie lay flat, heart thumping. It was too early for the SAS – it had to be Hugo and his stupid heroics. Her guess was confirmed when the doors were pushed open and two men came in dragging Hugo between them, his arms tied, blood trickling from his nose. The hostages around the walls of the room murmured in dismay.

'Silence!' barked Paschuk.

The men dropped Hugo on the floor at the general's feet and began a heated explanation of what had happened. When they'd finished, the general took up the baseball bat and turned to the captive, gaining his attention with a prod.

'Who are you?' he asked.

Hugo rolled to his knees. 'Hugo Kraus.'

'What are you doing here, Hugo Kraus? You were not on the guest list, nor are you a member of staff.'

'I wasn't doing anything.'

'So why were you in the basement with this?' Paschuk brandished the bat with skill; Darcie doubted he had learnt to handle it on the sport's field – torture chamber looked more likely to be his playground. 'Odd time for baseball practice.'

'I was just trying to get out. You've taken hostages – I was running for it.'

Paschuk tapped Hugo's shoulder. 'Through the basement? There's no way out from down there. Just the swimming pool.'

At that moment, the interview with Mrs Bridges

appeared again on the screen as part of the news loop. General Paschuk's expression changed. He scanned the faces of the hostages, then grabbed Hugo by the top of his head, bat under his chin, pressed against his throat.

'Who else is here?'

'No one,' gasped Hugo.

'The girl in the swimming pool – where is she?' He pushed Hugo aside and strode over to Jake. 'You!' he shouted, pointing with the bat. 'Your mother said your girlfriend is here. Where is she?'

'Girlfriend? I haven't got a girlfriend,' replied Jake, looking petrified.

'There was a girl with dark hair – I saw her swimming earlier – that woman . . .' he pointed to the television '. . . says you have a girlfriend here. Why isn't she here?'

'I don't know. Gone home?'

That was a mistake. Paschuk untied Jake and hauled him out next to Hugo. 'If any of you knows where the girl is hiding you are to tell me now or these boys die.' He clicked his fingers and the guns were aimed at Jake and Hugo. 'I will count to ten. If you haven't spoken up by then, I will order them to fire. One, two . . .'

Darcie felt paralyzed by terror. The hostages exchanged panicked glances.

'Three, four . . .'

Carmen stood up. 'There was a girl. But I haven't seen her since this afternoon. She must have gone home.'

Paschuk prodded her back down with the bat. 'Not good enough, Secretary General. I know she has not left – we were watching the gate all day. Five, six . . .'

Jake was shaking; Hugo scowled. Darcie could see her supposed comrade was trying to decide if he really wanted to lose his life to protect her. But then, could she stay hidden while they were shot in front of her eyes?

'Eight, nine . . .'

Darcie stood up, hands in the air. 'I'm here. Don't shoot.'

9

Paschuk clicked his fingers and the guns were lowered. 'So we have a spy, do we? Wait there.' He nodded to one of the men to fetch her. Darcie could feel all eyes fixed on her. She lowered her hands and slowly turned to the door, waiting for her escort to arrive. At the final moment, she thought to drop the phone into a potted palm. She'd suffered once already for possessing a phone fitted with a tracking device. The last thing she wanted was for Paschuk to examine her recent calls too closely.

Keep calm, she told herself. This will all be over at dawn. Just hang in there till then.

The guard, the stocky bronze-faced man with a droopy moustache she had noticed outside earlier in the day, seized her arm and marched her down to the hall. He forced her on to her knees next to Hugo and Jake.

'What's your name?' asked Paschuk, tipping her head up so he could look into her face.

'Darcie.'

He frowned. 'What are you doing here? You're not staff – you look no more than fifteen.'

'I'm fourteen. I'm on work experience.'

Paschuk gave a sceptical snort. 'You have gained more experience than you bargained for. Do not lie to me: you have been spying on us. What have you told the people outside?'

Darcie shook her head. 'Nothing – I've done nothing. I've just been hiding – I was scared.'

'So scared that you had to listen in on everything that was said in here?'

Darcie said no more: it had been a pretty lame story.

'In any case, it does not matter now. I have thought of a use for our three youngest guests. Secretary General?'

Carmen stood up. 'General Paschuk?'

'You have heard, of course, of the massacre of the villagers in Kutz? How the Russian army fired on a school, killing thirty children and their teachers?'

Carmen inclined her head.

'Tell me, what did the UN do?'

Carmen knew already before she opened her mouth that Paschuk would not be satisfied with her answer. 'We sent in a team of human rights monitors. We made vigorous protests to the Russian authorities.'

'Not vigorous enough. I am about to send them a warning – two of your young people will die because of what happened in Kutz. Any more casualties of Russian bullets and the third will suffer. Then you will all know what we felt at Kutz when we lost our children.'

Jake moaned and slumped forward, head in his hands. Desperate to reach his son, Kito Bridges shouted and surged up despite the ropes that bound him, but a gunman knocked him back, unconscious. Josephine screamed and rushed to cradle Kito in her lap, sobbing as she tried to revive him.

'No! You can't do that!' exclaimed Carmen, taking Paschuk's arm. 'You must know that two wrongs can never make a right. You claim the moral high ground from the Russians, but what you're doing here is as bad, if not worse, than your enemy. You are killing in cold blood!'

'I am only behaving as they have taught me.' Paschuk shook her off and strode over to Minister

Turgenov. He turned the Russian's white-thatched head roughly in direction of the three young people still kneeling on the ground. 'Take a good look, Turgenov. You are responsible for their deaths: remember their faces in the short time that you have left to you.' He motioned two of his men forward. 'As our hosts had the bad taste to bring us to a medieval castle and even gave us a tour – let us put it to proper use.' He pointed at Hugo and Darcie. 'Put those two in the death hole. Let them die slowly, memorably. Now if anyone else is listening, they will know I am serious. The boy,' he motioned to Jake, 'dies at dawn unless the Russian President goes on his knees to ask my forgiveness for the Kutz massacre.'

Numb with shock, Darcie allowed herself to be led away unresisting. Hugo put up more of a struggle and received more blows for his trouble. They were marched across the forecourt and into the dungeon tower. Half pushed, half stumbling down the stairs, Darcie was first to arrive at the open trapdoor leading to the death hole. She had not come down here before and she did not like what she saw. In the pit below, the stonework was slimy with seaweed and studded with barnacles; it obviously regularly spent time underwater. Six rusting chains were riveted to the wall, lapped by tiny waves as the tide seeped in.

Pushed from behind by the butt of a gun, Darcie tumbled ten feet into the waist-deep pool of water. Sand billowed around her as she struggled to the side. Hugo splashed in after her. The guards looked down on their two prisoners floundering below and began arguing as to which one would volunteer to chain them up. Neither wanted to get wet or risk another tussle with the blond boy. Deciding that it was unnecessary as the tide would do the job for them, they half-heartedly fired a few rounds into the water and slammed the trapdoor closed.

There had been only a few times in her life when Darcie had found herself in such complete darkness. She had to bite down on her knuckles to stop herself sobbing. Panic was not going to get them out of this.

Taking a gulp of air, she whispered, 'Are you all right, Hugo? They didn't get you?'

'No,' he replied gruffly.

She could hear his voice somewhere to her left. 'Where are you?' She felt out blindly with her arms.

'Here.' Her hands met his and she waded across to his side of the cell. She had never welcomed contact with Hugo, but now they needed each other. She kept hold of his hand.

'Ideas?' she asked, her voice shaking.

'Find a way out.' Hugo sounded reassuringly practical. If he wasn't going to panic, then she definitely wasn't going to disgrace herself in front of him. 'If you stand on my shoulders, Darcie, can you see if you can reach the trapdoor?'

He cradled his hands to give her a leg up. Darcie steadied herself against the wall as she got her balance.

'You'll have to move into the middle,' she said. 'The trap was near the centre of the ceiling.'

'Got you.'

He began to walk smoothly forward, holding her calves as she stretched to the ceiling like a circus acrobat. She could feel the roof – it seemed to be stone as was the rest of the cell – and it struck her that their prison was more like a cave hollowed out by the sea than something built by man. Perhaps the builders had broken through to it when digging the foundations of the tower?

'OK, stop there. I can feel the edge of the trap.' She pushed with all her might but it refused to budge. 'I can't move it.'

She heard Hugo cursing below. 'Try harder.'

'I am – really I am.'

Hugo's hands gripped her calves as he added his own push from below. They lost balance – Darcie tumbled from his shoulders, backwards into the water. He pulled her up by a handful of hair.

'Let go!' she spluttered. 'I'm all right.' She spat out a mouthful of seawater. 'I think it's locked. It seemed to give a fraction then stop as if there was a padlock or something keeping it closed.'

Hugo felt around the walls of the cell, rattling the manacles and brushing past Darcie in his search.

'What are you doing?' she asked through chattering teeth.

'Looking for something to force the lock – a rock, anything loose.'

Darcie joined the search, diving underwater to see if she could find anything on the sandy bottom. All she found was a pair of legs. She resurfaced.

'Keep going, I was enjoying that,' Hugo said with black humour. 'Found anything – other than my knees?'

'No. The floor's all sand – no big rocks. It seems to dip in the middle – sort of funnel-shaped. I guess the seawater comes in through a channel down there, but it's plugged with sand.'

'Can we dig out that way?'

'I tried but the sand kept slipping back in. Imagine trying to swim through that – we'd never manage it.'

Defeated for the moment, Hugo waded to the side. 'Let's take a break.'

There was nowhere dry to sit so they huddled together to keep warm.

'Not looking good, is it?' said Darcie.

'Not brilliant, no. Just now my cell in Kenya looks really inviting.'

Darcie had never bothered to ask herself what he had suffered after his arrest as she had been convinced he deserved every moment in jail. Now, trapped with him, very likely to die in his company, she found herself wondering what prison had done to him.

'What was it like – in Kenya, I mean?' Darcie asked.

She felt him stiffen. 'Not much to tell. I was really angry most of the time.'

'Angry? With me?'

'Yes,' he admitted, 'but also really hacked off with my father.'

'You tried to kill me, Hugo. I never tried to kill you.'

'I can see from your point of view that I deserved my punishment,' he conceded.

'And from your point of view – what about that?'

He sighed, relaxing a little. 'I don't know now. I suppose I feel that none of it was worth it. I was doing well at school – I even liked it. I had some cool friends, time for a laugh, fun at the weekends. I could have been anything I wanted, gone anywhere, but I suppose we tried to take a few shortcuts. It was a gamble – we lost. I regret missing out on all that normal stuff – university, being free to make my own choices.' He fell silent, perhaps aware he'd revealed too much. When he started talking again, his tone was much brisker. 'So what? Things move on: someone else is using me and I've no idea what my life is going to be like now Gladys Smith has got me. I don't even know if I believe in any of the things she stands for – Queen and country – that stuff.'

The water had reached Darcie's chest. 'You may not have to worry about it. I doubt anyone will come in time to save us for you to find out what you believe in.'

'That's all right then.' He gave a bark of desperate laughter. 'You know, Darcie, you're not exactly my first choice of a companion in death.'

'You neither.'

'I still don't like you.' Without asking permission, he lifted her on to his shoulders so she was clear of the water.

'Same here.'

'You're not going to go to pieces on me. I don't want to spend my last minutes on earth with you snivelling in my hair.'

'How do you want to spend your last minutes then?' She was shivering – he must be able to feel it.

'I dunno. Not given it much thought.'

The water seemed to be coming in much faster now. It was pooling around her knees, which meant it was up to Hugo's neck.

'You'd better let me down so you can swim.' She slid from his back but they didn't let go of each other. Neither wanted to die alone in the darkness.

Suddenly, Hugo punched the water. 'I know!'

'What?'

'I know how I want to spend my last moments. I want to kiss you.'

'What?'

'Yeah, why not? You've nothing to lose. You won't have to live with yourself afterwards and it'll make me feel a lot better. One mission accomplished even if the rest is a failure.'

'What mission?'

Hugo gave a hollow laugh. 'I had a bet with myself back in Nairobi that I could get you to kiss me. I've gone rather to the extreme, don't you think, getting you down here with me? At least I deserve a reward for single-minded persistence.'

Darcie was now treading water in the dark pool, feeling the sand swirl around her.

'You're mad, Hugo.'

'Yeah, probably. Go on: make a dying boy happy.'

Darcie wavered but, at that moment, she felt a sudden rush of cold water around her feet. The manacles clanked on the wall as the current stirred them.

'I don't know about you, Hugo, but I'm not ready to die just yet – and I'm not quite desperate enough to kiss you.'

She flipped up and dived to the floor, groping for the dip she had found earlier. It had dawned on her why there were chains in a supposedly secure room – a waste if the prisoners would drown anyway when the tide reached the ceiling. Perhaps, just perhaps, the sand plug was exactly that: a plug that was pushed out when the tide reached a certain height, only resettling as the water drained away. It was too dark to make out anything in the murk so Darcie followed the current and found the source pouring in through a hole at the base of one wall. Sand was everywhere, no longer packed down but floating free in the incoming tide. This was their only chance.

She burst back to the surface.

'I think there's a way out – but it's very narrow,' she gasped.

'Yes!' Hugo crowed in relief. 'Do you want me to try it?' Without waiting for an answer, Hugo took a breath in preparation to dive.

'No!' Darcie caught him by the shirt. 'No offence, Hugo, but it feels too narrow for you.'

'I can't let a girl take a risk for me.'

'It's not about heroics: I'm thinking of myself. If you go and get stuck in it then I'd be trapped. If I get through, I'll come and get you out. It's our best chance.'

He didn't believe her but dived under the water to check out the gap for himself. Darcie waited a few anxious moments, praying he hadn't gone ahead anyway. She sighed with relief when he broke the surface.

'OK: you try. Don't forget me, will you?' He said it jokily, but there was an edge of panic in his voice.

'Would I ever?'

She took off her shoes and passed them to him. Taking a few deep breaths to get as much oxygen in her system as possible, Darcie dived down again. She found the gap quickly this time and used the lip of rock to pull herself into it. Water pushed against her as she hauled herself along the narrow submerged passage. She tried not to think of what would happen if she got stuck – there could be no death lonelier than this one – but she struggled on. The tide had to be coming from somewhere.

Her lungs were now burning as she found the passage walls widen on either side out of her reach. She kicked upwards – only to bump the top of her head. Too soon. Trying to ignore a rising bubble of panic, she made a few more strokes. She could now sense more clearly the tug and push of the waves but her strength was failing. Breathe, screamed her lungs as a creeping darkness began to spread over her mind. She could feel herself beginning to black out as her body shut down. With one final effort, she gave a great kick, using the momentum of the retreating wave to pull her forward, swim up – and burst into wonderful, glorious fresh air.

Now, breathe! she told her oxygen-starved body. She had survived. Limply, she floated in the water, unable to move, her heart still pounding after the close call in the tunnel.

Her relief was cut rudely short. An incoming

wave picked her up and threw her against the cliff. Her head cracked against rock, elbows scraped. She had to get away from here before the next wave struck. Oxygen flowing once more, she swam with the backwash, diving through the next wave and distancing herself from the sheer cliff face. Pausing to tread water for a moment, she could hear the surf breaking on the beach. It couldn't be far. Rounding the headland, she spotted the same rock she had climbed on only yesterday, though that now seemed an age ago. Swimming to its base, she clung to it, snatching a brief rest. She had to hurry or Hugo would be out of air. The beach seemed empty, eerily quiet considering what was going on inside St Helen's. She had hoped that the rescue team might have got this close already, but Paschuk had warned he would start shooting if he saw any activity outside – the authorities had obviously taken him seriously. She had to assume she was on her own.

Darcie swam to the beach and staggered out of the water, exhaustion beginning to catch up with her. She rubbed her arms vigorously: she did not have time to collapse on the sand as she would have liked. A trickle of blood leaked down her cheek from where her head had hit the rock; she was lucky she hadn't been knocked out. If it had been a stormy day, she wouldn't have stood a chance.

Stumbling to the steps zigzagging up from the beach, she began her weary ascent, trying to hurry even though her legs were like lead. She paused at every turn, listening. Nothing.

She had almost reached the top when the sound she most feared reached her: footsteps. Ducking down, she crouched by the cliff face, praying the Tazbeks would not bother to patrol down here. Above she caught the firefly glimmer of a cigarette flaring briefly in the dark.

How long can it take someone to smoke a cigarette? These Tazbeks must be chain-smokers – they never seemed to be without one in their fingers. The safest thing would be to stay here until the guard finished and let Hugo take his chances with the tide.

But you promised not to forget him. What if delaying here means he's dead when you open the trapdoor?

Darcie swore at her conscience, which had inconveniently stepped into the debate. She knew she wouldn't be able to live with herself if she stood by and let Hugo drown without even trying.

Picking a heavy stone off a ledge, she threw it as

hard as she could on to the stairs. It bumped and clattered from step to step. Cigarette thrown aside, the guard shouted a challenge.

Silence.

Had she done enough? Probably not. She took a handful of pebbles and threw them on to the beach. The safety catch of the man's gun clicked. He peered over the rail, trying to make out what was happening below. Darcie could almost hear him thinking: report in or investigate? She willed him to go and fetch reinforcements.

She lost the gamble. The guard began to descend the steps at the double. He would be upon her any moment and she had nowhere to run. Terrified, Darcie curled up in a ball. He was near her now – she could hear his panting breath. A foot struck her hip. Something heavy tumbled over her back, but continued falling; a gun flew into the air and smashed onto the rocks below. Darcie sprang to her feet. At the foot of the stairs, a man's body lay crumpled at a strange angle.

She'd killed him. By accident, but she had killed him. He had never even seen her hidden there in the shadow of the cliff and had tripped right over her.

Darcie gripped the rail, shaking as she looked

down on the dead man. She supposed she should be relieved – but all she felt was horror.

Hugo.

The thought of what might be happening to him galvanized her into action. She would think about this later – right now she had to save Hugo.

Darcie ran up the steps and tried the door under the archway leading into the dungeon tower. Luck was with her: it was open. She clattered down the spiral stone stair to the trapdoor. Her panic rose again, filling her mouth with a bitter taste: she could hear the slosh of waves against the trap – she was too late.

'Hugo!' she screamed. 'Hugo!' The answer was a thump on the door below. Springing into action, she tugged on the ring handle.

The trap was padlocked as she had guessed. Darcie pulled but it was firm – a new lock, shiny and bright in the glow of the bare bulb dangling from the ceiling. Close to despair, Darcie searched for something to smash the door, but there was nothing.

Then she saw the key, hanging innocently on a hook by the light switch. There had been no reason to hide it. No one expected a rescue attempt. Fumbling with cold fingers, she undid the padlock and heaved the trap open. Hugo reached up – there were only inches of air left between the water and the ceiling. Darcie grasped his wrists and pulled. He slithered out and collapsed in a heap.

'You took your time,' he coughed, chucking her shoes at her.

Darcie felt like kicking him for his ingratitude.

'Come on,' she said testily, slipping her trainers back on. 'We're not safe here. By the looks of things, the tide rises up these steps too.' The walls were stained green at the bottom and the whole place had a dank, wet smell.

Hugo staggered to his feet and caught her by the back of her T-shirt before she could leave.

'I need a hug.'

'Get lost.' She tried to push him back but he grabbed her to him. He was very cold.

'No, I mean it. I thought I was dead – I thought you'd drowned, or left me on purpose.' He was shaking, white with shock. For the first time since she met him, he looked vulnerable.

'Well, you're not dead – neither am I.' She remembered with a sick feeling the man at the bottom of the stairs and disentangled herself. 'But I killed one of them to get to you so they'll soon work out that someone's here. We've got to hide.'

Recovering slightly, Hugo squared his shoulders.

He looked at her with a new respect just as she felt most disgusted with herself. 'I didn't think you had it in you.'

'I don't. It was an accident. Now shut up about that and come on.'

'Where are we going?' he asked as they began to mount the stairs.

'I don't know,' Darcie admitted. If she had it her way, they'd run and run until they made it out of there, but she could not forget the fact that Jake was the next one to die according to Paschuk. The general might carry out his threat before the rescue team got here. She had at least to brief her dad as to what was happening, try and persuade them to bring the rescue forward a few hours.

And that meant returning to her phone.

'We're going back inside – I know another way in,' she told Hugo.

'You are full of surprises. I was betting that you were going to run for it. But I like it: we'll take the fight to them. They think we're dead so they won't be expecting that.'

'I've no intention of starting a fight with anyone. We're going back to get more orders from Mrs Smith and tell her about Jake.'

'Oh, trying to save the boyfriend: now I understand. OK, boss, let's do it.'

He pushed past her on the stairs. It hadn't taken him long to return to his old infuriating ways. She preferred him half-drowned and scared.

10

Carmen Lopez had spent the last hour eaten up with an agony of grief and rage such as she had never known in all her long and varied career. She could not tear her thoughts away from the fate that had befallen Darcie and Hugo. She had begged General Paschuk to let her take their place, pleaded for mercy, even railed at Paschuk for his cruelty, but nothing had any effect. Exhausted, Carmen now sat with her head on her knees, wishing she had never stepped foot in St Helen's – she had brought nothing but trouble upon this place with her high-minded but unrealistic ambitions to bring peace.

'Please, ma'am?' It was the cook, Josephine, whispering in a voice cracked with fear. 'Can't you do something to save our boy?'

Carmen raised her eyes and saw Jake still on his knees, hands behind his head, gun pointing at him. Though his face glistened with tears, his courage was clear in the firm set of his shoulders; he had not tried to plead or beg, but shamed his captors with his dignified silence. She felt overwhelmed with hopelessness: another innocent victim lined up before them and with all her supposed power and influence, the might of the United Nations behind her, she could do nothing.

Rage gained the upper hand. She had not dragged herself out of the slums to end it like this. Carmen jumped to her feet and marched over to Paschuk.

'You are a coward!' she spat, arms on her hips as she bristled with anger. 'You have a grievance? Settle it like a man and don't pick on the children.'

A deathly silence fell as Paschuk muted the sound on the television and turned to her, his disdain evident in the set of his curled lips.

'What, Secretary General, have we lost our diplomatic cool?' he mocked.

'Yes, we have. I never rated diplomatic cool very highly in the first place. Sometimes people need to hear the truth.' She pointed with a quivering finger at Jake. 'This boy – those two you've murdered – what have they done to you? Nothing. If you're angry, take it out on your enemies – on the United Nations if you must – but not on English school children who probably couldn't even find Tazbekistan on the map. They are not part of this.'

Paschuk's eyes blazed at the idea that his country could be so insignificant to someone else. 'If you carry on like this, Secretary General, I will have to have you gagged.'

'So you would silence the truth, would you?'

'You bore me.' He waved her back to her seat. 'I'm not interested in your preaching.'

Carmen drew herself up to her full height of five feet five inches, and slapped him hard across the face. 'That's what you deserve, you pig!'

Paschuk rubbed his cheek reflectively for a moment, his expression wavering between outrage and amusement, then he burst into a roar of laughter. 'You are a brave but stupid woman, Secretary General. Sit down.'

John Riddell watched with horrified admiration as Carmen stalked back to her place. His own brand of diplomacy had always been of the quiet, behind the scenes sort: he had never slapped anyone though he had often been tempted to knock heads together. Her bravery boosted his courage, reminding him of his student days confronting the authorities on the picket lines. He'd never been one to give in without a protest.

'General Paschuk!' he called. He could not get up as he was still tied to the Russian minister, Turgenov.

'Foreign Secretary,' Paschuk said wearily. 'Not another intervention? I hope you have something more constructive to say?'

'You must be hoping for a negotiated end to this siege?'

Paschuk gave a crooked smile. 'I do not have a death wish, if that is what you mean, though I am fully prepared to die for my country.'

'And we already know that you will kill for it. The murders of two innocents is two too many. You have made your point – let the boy go and then we can discuss how to resolve this crisis. You must realise that my government takes a robust view of hostage situations – far better to end this peacefully with no more loss of life.'

Paschuk checked his watch. 'Look at that: it is high tide. I think it is a good time to contact the outside world. Perhaps, Mr Riddell, you would like to be the bearer of bad tidings to your people. That should convince them that I'm serious. Any delay, any prevarication, then a third child will be sacrificed.'

He gave a nod to one of his men and Riddell was untied and marched into the entrance hall. Paschuk stood at his shoulder and pointed to the phone.

'I presume you know the prime minister's number?' he said coldly.

A phone rang at the prime minister's right hand in the crisis meeting room. The people around the table fell silent – it was the line dedicated to the hostage situation. The prime minister snatched it up, already sweating heavily.

'John? Are you all right?'

Christopher Lock wished the PM would put the call on speakerphone so they could all listen in, but he didn't. He listened carefully, nodding twice, his face ashen. Once his eyes flicked over to Christopher Lock, but otherwise he kept his gaze on his pad as he jotted down notes. Finally, he put the phone down and cleared his throat.

'I'm afraid it's very bad news. We've lost two of our people. The killing has started and a third child is being threatened.'

'A third child?' Christopher queried. 'So does that mean –?'

'Yes, two have already been brutally murdered.' Christopher went still, his fingers frozen to his pen. The prime minister looked over at him. 'I'm sorry, Christopher, but one of them was Darcie. The other a boy called Hugo Kraus. They were drowned together in some god-awful stunt dreamt up by Paschuk.'

Darcie's grandfather picked up his glass, his hand shaking as he took a sip. Everyone was looking at him. But it couldn't be true. They had thought she was dead before and been wrong.

'Maybe there is a mistake,' he said hoarsely.

'I'm sorry but there's no mistake. John spoke to Darcie only this afternoon and saw her led away. It was definitely her. She was caught listening on the balcony. I take it she was there on your orders?'

Christopher nodded.

'Then she was a very brave girl. We understand if you need to go, Christopher. But for the rest of us, we still have a crisis to deal with.'

Staring at his hands, Christopher felt his self-deceptions crumble about him. His skin was wrinkled and old, so old, his fingers trembling: he was losing his touch, fatally misreading situations. He had fooled himself into believing her youth would protect her. Another Christopher Lock masterstroke. But he should have known better. He should offer his resignation here and now before he made any more mistakes.

The phone rang again. The prime minister picked it up, face set against yet more bad news. Suddenly, he broke into an incredulous grin and punched the speakerphone setting.

'Er, hi, it's Darcie Lock here. Can I speak to my grandfather?'

Darcie was crouched down in the kitchens behind the chest freezer. Hugo was on lookout. He had promised that he would take no risks. They had got this far by climbing in over the wheelie bins and through the back door. Darcie had then ransacked Jake's bag for his phone. Not knowing the number for Stingo or her father by heart she had been forced to dial 999. She had spent five infuriating minutes persuading the switchboard operator that this was not a hoax, then found herself passed from one Whitehall department to another, until finally they had connected her to the prime minister's direct line. She had no idea that half the cabinet were in the room too.

'Darcie, you're alive!' her grandfather exclaimed, relief nearly choking him.

'Only just. I'm afraid I killed one of the Tazbeks in the process so they'll soon know we got out.'

'You said "we". So Hugo's there too?'

'Yeah. He's just checking outside. I'm in the back kitchen.'

The prime minister's aide clicked up the map of St Helen's on a display and highlighted Darcie's position.

'What can you tell us? Any change inside?'

There was the sound of fumbling and then Hugo came on the line. 'Sir, I've just discovered that the enemy is booby-trapping the building. I saw one of them rigging up explosives around the hall where the hostages are being held.'

'Where the hell did they get explosives from!' muttered the prime minister. 'Don't tell me: it's a training college – you keep the stuff on site?'

Christopher gave a curt nod but continued speaking to Hugo. 'That complicates things, though not surprising. Paschuk knows his strategy. He's trying to prevent any attempt to end the siege by force.'

'Correct, sir,' agreed Hugo. 'It's what I would do in his shoes.'

'Wait there for further orders, Kraus. Can I speak to Darcie for a moment?'

'Grandfather?'

'I . . . I'm very glad you're alive. Keep it that way.' It was the closest he could bring himself to telling her that he loved her.

'I'll try.'

'Stand by for more orders.'

'OK.'

'Do you think we're safe here?' Darcie whispered. The larder had only a tiny window and with the door closed it was unlikely they would think to look in here. But after the death hole, she had an aversion to being boxed in.

Hugo shrugged. 'I dunno. There seems to be an external patrol, the man laying the traps, a couple in with Paschuk. I suppose someone's down in the basement with our guys. How many does that make?'

'Eight? Nine?'

'Yeah, about that.' He thumped his head back against the wall. 'I'm sure we could take them. I mean you've already got rid of one for us.'

Darcie shuddered. 'By accident. He tripped over

me and fell down the cliff.'

'Better him with a broken neck than you.' Hugo couldn't understand her squeamishness. 'I'll say one thing for you, Darcie: you may not be very good at this stuff, but at least you're lucky.'

She closed her eyes, conscious of how wet and tired she was. Her spirits had sunk low; by contrast, now he was no longer drowning, Hugo seemed to be enjoying himself. She heard him get up and rummage through the contents of the shelves. Something dropped into her lap.

'Eat,' said Hugo. 'We need to keep up our energy levels. Anyway, no point letting it all go to waste.'

Darcie found a slab of salmon wedged between two rolls in her lap – spoils from the banquet that never got served. She realised how hungry she was and took several large bites, forcing herself to swallow. Hugo chucked her a bottle of mineral water to wash it all down.

'Now, let's have a look at your head,' Hugo said, brushing the crumbs from his hands.

'It's fine.'

'Doesn't look fine. An injury can slow your team – it's policy to treat it as soon as possible.'

He seized her chin and turned her face to the light. 'How did you do it?'

'Hit the rocks when I swam out.'

Grabbing a fistful of serviettes, Hugo splashed some mineral water on the wad and dabbed her temple. The blood that had dried on the wound wiped away, the injury began to ooze again.

'You'll need a stitch on that, I think.'

'Don't you dare!' Darcie flinched away from him.

He grinned. 'Tempting though it would be to inflict pain on you – even I can't sew a wound up with breadsticks. You'll have to manage for now.'

Jake's phone vibrated. They both made a grab for it, but Hugo won. 'Who? Warrant Officer Galt? Oh yeah, I remember. Yeah, Darcie's here.' Hugo passed her the phone. 'Wants to talk to you. Said he doesn't like me for some reason.'

'Would that be because you shot him?' Darcie asked sardonically. 'Hi, Stingo.'

'Darcie, Gladys Smith and I have been put in charge of liaison with you for the next stage,' said Stingo, speaking rapidly in what she recognized as his professional voice.

'What's the next stage?'

'We're changing our plans. It's been decided that a full-out assault would trigger the booby-traps – Paschuk is clearly not intending to be taken alive if we storm the place. We don't care about him but it would lead to unacceptable civilian losses.'

'I suppose no one's suggested giving him what he wants?'

'You tell that to the Russians.'

'OK. Fine. What do you want us to do?' Darcie could feel some of her tension unwinding. She'd been in worse spots with Stingo and he'd always got her out; he'd know exactly what to do.

'The team's going to try and infiltrate your base without alerting Paschuk. We must get into the building – he doesn't have enough men to guard all entry points at all times. But to do this successfully, we need him to be distracted.'

'How?'

'The theory is that if we can't do it from the outside without triggering more hostage killings, we need to do it from the inside.'

'Go on.'

'We want you and Hugo to arrange for the Tazbeks to be confused – bothered. Lots of little stings – no big hits. We don't want them to take it as a challenge. Something subtle. While they're chasing the ghosts in the machine, we'll try and get in.'

Darcie felt her heart leap. 'You're coming in?'

'Not me. I'm at our HQ as I know all the players.

It'll be the rest of the squad.'

Darcie tried to ignore her disappointment; as much as she liked the men in the squad, they weren't the same as Stingo. 'OK. Is that it?'

'Yes. Maximum disruption without being caught: those are your orders. Mrs Smith is putting you in charge, got that? We trust your judgement to get it right. Mrs Smith wants to speak to Kraus for a moment.'

Darcie passed the phone to Hugo.

'Hugo?'

'Ma'am?'

Mrs Smith's voice had its customary cool and unruffled tone. 'Take Darcie's lead from now on. She's senior officer on this operation.'

'But, ma'am, Darcie is –'

'Is what? Younger than you? A girl? What's your problem, Hugo?'

'She's . . . too cautious. Hasn't got the guts for this work.'

Stingo grabbed the phone back from Mrs Smith. 'Listen, you disgusting toe-rag, Darcie is braver and smarter than you. She's also more experienced. Follow her orders.'

'Sir.'

'And if I hear that you've harmed a hair on her

head, or let someone else harm her, then I will personally hunt you down and take you apart piece by piece. Got that?'

'Yes, sir.' Hugo grimaced. 'Over and out.'

Operation Ghost-in-the-Machine started in the kitchen. Darcie put a chip pan on the cooker, gas on high; Hugo blocked the plughole and turned the taps on full.

'Fire, oil and water – this should be interesting,' he commented. 'How long till they notice, do you think?'

'Five, ten minutes, I guess. Where next?'

'You're the boss.'

'Oh.' Darcie was taken aback by his submissive attitude. 'Well, I had one idea that'll keep the patrol busy but we need to get round each of the bedrooms without being seen.'

'Wait till they start fighting the fire then – that'll take most of the guys on the inside.' Hugo put a fire extinguisher on the side. 'As we don't actually want to burn the place down with a load of explosives inside, I'll leave this here.'

They climbed back over the wheelie bins and crept around to the library window. Through the lighted room they could see the entrance hall and beyond that the closed doors of the dining hall. They crouched either side in the shrubbery and waited. Six minutes later the fire alarms were triggered, starting on the ground floor but rapidly passing throughout the building. Two men ran down the stairs from the upper floor and disappeared into the kitchens. Darcie was pleased to see a black cloud of smoke belch from the corridor. Water leaked along the floor.

'Go!' Darcie whispered.

They rushed in through the French windows and bolted up the stairs. Rapidly they passed through the bedrooms, repeating the same task in each.

'Let's shift a few things about,' suggested Hugo, heaving the suit of armour out of its cubbyhole and placing it in the centre of the corridor. Darcie immediately followed by balancing a flower arrangement precariously on the banister. They took pictures from the wall, spread mops and laundry in the way, and finally turned the taps on in all the bathrooms.

'Retreat?' asked Hugo, breathing heavily after having shifted a wardrobe so it would crash over when his bedroom door was opened.

Darcie nodded. They pushed open the attic. Hugo went first. Darcie moved the table he had used back against the wall, then jumped up so he could pull her in.

'Much easier with two,' she said, collapsing on a pile of old curtains.

'What now?'

'And now we wait. I'll check in and tell them what we've done.'

'Idiots!' Paschuk bellowed at his men as they returned from the kitchen fire. You should've checked everything was secure when you brought the staff in here!' Anger flaring like the chip pan, he struck one junior around the face.

The young man glared at him mutinously. 'But, General, we did!' he protested.

'Where's the chef?' Paschuk wheeled round on the hostages, searching for someone else to take the brunt of his rage.

Jake steeled himself to act: no way was he going to let anyone hurt his father – not after losing Darcie.

Just then a beeping began in the hall outside.

'What now?' barked Paschuk. Beginning to think that he was surrounded by imbeciles, he strode out to investigate for himself. The sound was coming from upstairs – beeping, voices burbling, music – as one by one the radio alarm clocks at each bedside switched themselves on at full volume. He came back into the hall and clicked his fingers at two of his men.

'You and you! Go and turn those damn things off and search the place properly this time.'

Most of the hostages understood nothing of what was being said but the Russians and Tazbek civilians whispered translations to those around them. Jake took heart – he couldn't understand what was going on but it appeared that the house itself was coming out on their side. The hostages waited in silence. There was a crash and a curse from the entrance hall as a vase of flowers fell from the banister. Next came an almighty noise like a rumble of thunder as a suit of armour tumbled down the stairs. Paschuk's frown deepened so that the creases on his brow looked like knife cuts. Maddened by these petty irritations, the guards took their revenge and, one by one, clock radios were silenced as the soldiers ripped them from the walls or smashed them with rifle butts. There was a final bang from the top floor as a wardrobe almost crushed the man attempting to enter Hugo's room.

The two men returned to the hall, breathless and

spooked.

'There's no one up there, general,' they reported, 'but this place seems to have a mind of its own.'

Paschuk's eyes swept the row of bedraggled hostages. He swooped on James Harlem, the man he had tagged as the organiser, dragging him out next to Jake. Jake could sense the man's terror, but he was holding his nerve.

'You! Tell me what's going on.'

'I don't know, General,' James replied truthfully, face grey with fear.

'You lie. These things cannot happen by themselves.'

James licked his dry lips nervously. 'Coincidence perhaps? Someone's idea of a practical joke before all this started?'

Carmen had been thinking fast. It seemed clear to her that there were unknown allies in the building. What they were attempting to achieve with their little stunts, she could not imagine, but it had the Tazbeks on edge. Instinctively, she knew it was best if Paschuk did not think along these lines.

She stood up. 'Yes, that's right. I'm afraid it was me. I thought earlier to play a joke on you all – in poor taste I see now. I had completely forgotten what I'd done.'

Paschuk stared at her. Carmen Lopez had a reputation for unpredictability but this was bizarre even for her.

'A joke?'

'Yes.' Carmen glanced at her watch – it was three in the morning. 'I thought it would get everyone out of bed and we could have a pyjama party – you know, break the ice.'

'Secretary General,' spat Paschuk, 'I have long thought you to be unworthy of the office you hold, but this . . . this is . . .'

Carmen never found out what 'this' was as a chunk of plaster gave way in the ceiling at the far end of the hall and crashed to the floor. Water poured in from the bathroom above.

'I think we have a burst pipe,' Carmen said dryly.

Jake would have cheered her cool if he hadn't been so terrified for her safety.

Paschuk grabbed Carmen's arm and dragged her to the centre of the room.

'Deal with it!' he ordered his men, jerking his head at the water. 'Then take this place apart bit by bit until you find who's behind this!' He turned back to Carmen, his eyes murderous. 'As for you, Madam Lopez, I think it is time we had a new secretary general, don't you?' He reached for his revolver and raised it to her head. Carmen met his gaze, determined to die with her head held high.

'No!' Suddenly, to Jake's left, James Harlem leapt up and butted Paschuk in the stomach, forcing himself between the gun and Carmen. A shot was fired and James fell to the floor, blood pouring from a wound in his side. Panic erupted in the room as the hostages screamed and yelled. Frozen for just an instant, Jake crawled to James's side and clamped his hands over the wound, trying to exert pressure to stop the bleeding. Carmen dropped to her knees, joining him in the attempt to staunch the flow, using the hem of her red dress as a makeshift bandage. Paschuk fired a shot into the air. All went silent except for the private secretary, who was moaning with pain.

'Stay with us,' murmured Jake. 'You'll be OK. Just stay with us.'

General Paschuk glanced at his victim in disgust as the young man stained the ancient flagstones with his blood. 'I won't waste another bullet on him. Take him outside. You,' he nodded at John Riddell, 'you can tell your people to send two unarmed stretcher bearers to take him away. If you try anything, I'll shoot him like a dog.'

11

Darcie could hear the men below upending beds and overturning furniture.

'How long before they think to look up here?' she whispered to Hugo.

Not long was the answer. One of the Tazbeks turned his gun to the ceiling and fired a spray of bullets upwards. The shots exploded through the attic a few metres from their position. It took all of Darcie's restraint not to cry out in terror.

Hugo nodded to the far end. 'We'd better get out.'

They crept away from the hatch to the far wall. There was no escape that Darcie could see but Hugo was not deterred. He tore away the insulating felt and then lashed out with his foot to kick a hole in the tiles and wooden supports. Once it was big enough, he slithered out on to the rooftop and disappeared from sight. Darcie did not have long to hesitate as there were thumps on the attic door – the Tazbeks had worked out the hiding place. She climbed through the hole, legs first, and slid down to the gutter. Hugo caught the back of her shirt to stop her tumbling over the edge. He had wedged himself against the crenella-tions that disguised the gutter running along the roof edge. It was quite broad, easy enough to walk along; the only problem was where to go from here.

'They're coming,' Darcie told Hugo. 'Let's go.'

Peering over the edge they saw that they were three storeys up.

'We'll have to climb down that,' Hugo announced, pointing to a black iron drainpipe.

'You can if you want – but I'd rather find the fire escape,' said Darcie, making her way carefully along the gutter.

He frowned. 'What fire escape?'

'Don't you ever read the fire safety cards in hotel rooms?' She crept round the corner and found what she was looking for – an iron staircase zigzagging down the side of the building – ugly, but at that moment to her eyes, it was the most wonderful thing she had ever seen.

Hugo went first, dropping the two metres from the edge of the roof on to the iron gantry. Darcie followed, trying not to make too much noise as she landed. Both knew that as soon as the Tazbeks found the hole in the roof, the search would move to the exterior of the building.

'Have we done enough?' panted Hugo when they reached the ground. 'Or do we go back in?'

Darcie had had another idea. 'Car park,' she said, and set off at a run for the bushes, taking it for granted that Hugo would follow her lead. It was bizarre, but despite her fear, she was enjoying herself.

Making their way around to the rear of the building, they found the courtyard full of vehicles – technicians' lorries, the caterers' vans and the diplomatic cars.

'What now?' asked Hugo.

'Set off the car alarms and run for it.'

'Run where?'

Darcie grimaced. 'You are allowed to make suggestions, you know. You've been here longer than me.'

'Firing range. They've cleaned it out, so I expect

they won't waste a man guarding it, and I know it well.'

'OK. You take the vehicles on that side; I'll do the others. Then make your own way to the range for cover. We'll meet there in ten minutes. If either of us gets caught, the other didn't make it out of the dungeon, agreed?'

He nodded, bracing himself for the quick dash across the open.

'Wait!' Darcie grabbed him, spotting movement outside the building. Two stretcher bearers were carrying a body towards a parked ambulance – she couldn't tell from this distance if they were alive or dead.

'Who do you think that is?' Hugo whispered.

Darcie shook her head. Not Jake, please let it not be Jake.

They waited until the ambulance had driven out of sight.

'Go!' Darcie pushed Hugo up as she began her own sprint forwards. Taking a jump on to the bonnet of the nearest limousine, she ran the length of the car and leapt off the other end. As she expected, the impact was enough to set off the wail of the alarm. In the glow of flashing sidelights, she tackled two more cars in the same way, then picked up a flowerpot and threw it at the catering van. The noise built to a crescendo, tearing at the eardrums. Not something the Tazbeks could ignore.

Job done, Darcie dashed for cover in the bushes. She saw Hugo give a final kick to a stubbornly silent car before he realised that it wasn't fitted with an alarm. He dived out of sight just in time. Two Tazbeks ran around the corner of the building, then pulled up short, confused by the courtyard of demented vehicles. Rather pointlessly, in Darcie's estimation, one squeezed the trigger and shot the nearest car in anger. All he succeeded in doing was setting off the alarm in a car that Darcie had missed.

Allowing herself a small smile of self-congratulation, Darcie began to move backwards deeper into the shrubbery. If this didn't provide sufficient distraction for the rescue team, then she didn't know what would.

Her progress halted when she felt the cold touch of steel on the back of her neck. A hand gripped her shoulder and turned her around. Looking up, she found herself staring into the eyes of General Paschuk.

'You!' he spat. 'Where is the other?'

Darcie gulped. 'He . . . he drowned. I swam out but he got stuck in the tunnel.'

Paschuk's eyes narrowed, clearly wondering if he could believe her.

'Come!' he barked. Shouting an order to the men in the car park, he dragged her with him back into the house.

Darcie knew she should be thankful he hadn't shot her on the spot, but it was particularly galling to be back at square one with all the other hostages after having enjoyed a brief moment of freedom. She refused to wonder what he would do with her now: none of her guesses were encouraging.

Her appearance in the hall was met with astonished exclamations from the other captives.

'Darcie!' Jake made a move towards her but was pushed back by his guard.

'My God, are you all right?' asked John Riddell. It seemed a foolish question when she had dried blood smeared across her cheek from a head wound and a gun pointing at her.

'Yes,' she replied.

'The boy?'

She shook her head, hoping to convince the Tazbeks that there was no one else at large. 'Didn't make it.'

Paschuk forced Darcie on to her knees. 'You!' He

pointed the muzzle of his gun at John Riddell. 'Shut up! You,' he gestured to Darcie, 'talk. Why?'

Darcie couldn't think of a plausible excuse. 'I . . . I . . .' Her training in Nairobi came back to her: do the unexpected, make your attacker underestimate you. 'I think I'm going to faint.' Clutching her head, she crumpled.

Carmen started forward. 'The girl's injured, General Paschuk. How can you interrogate her in this state? She needs a doctor.'

Paschuk gave a disgusted grunt. 'Bring her round, Secretary General. She has answers I want.'

Darcie heard the whisper of silk and caught a whiff of expensive perfume. Cool hands gently lifted her head off the floor.

'I need better light. I can't see how badly hurt she is,' Carmen announced.

Paschuk clicked his fingers at Riddell and Turgenov. 'Carry the girl into the office across the hall.' He then continued his orders in Russian to the men on guard. One came forward to untie the two ministers.

With a glance at each other, Riddell and Turgenov picked up their burden and shuffled from the entrance hall to the housekeeper's office. Putting her down carefully on a sofa under the window, Riddell muttered, 'I'd stay like that, if I were you.'

Darcie risked opening her eyes a crack. Paschuk was not yet in the room. 'Rescue team coming very soon,' she whispered. 'Be ready.'

Riddell nodded.

'What she say?' asked Turgenov urgently. Riddell hushed him as Paschuk strode in, bringing Jake and Carmen with him.

'You two, back to the hall. I want a word in private with the secretary general and the young people.' Paschuk emphasized his words by waving his gun to the door. Darcie heard the two men retreat and the door close. Silence.

'Bring her round,' Paschuk ordered Carmen. 'And let her know that if she doesn't wake up, I will shoot the boy.'

'That's ridiculous, General. The girl can't regain consciousness to order!' protested Carmen.

'Do it!'

Carmen lightly slapped Darcie's cheeks. 'Come on, sweetheart, time to rejoin the living.'

Knowing she had little option but to rouse herself, Darcie faked her recovery.

'I feel sick,' she groaned, rolling so as to hang half off the sofa. The position gave her a good view of Carmen's delicate bracelet watch. 4.30. The rescue team should be here any moment now. They just had to hold on a little longer.

'You have caused me a lot of trouble,' Paschuk began. He motioned Carmen and Jake to sit beside Darcie on the sofa. He sat on the edge of the desk, keeping them covered by his weapon at all times.

Darcie said nothing, her gaze on her grazed knuckles clenched in her lap. Come on, come on, she urged the rescue party. She could feel Jake sitting tensely on her left; he reached between them, letting his fingers touch her leg briefly.

'Tell me how you got out of the cell,' Paschuk demanded.

Darcie licked her dry lips. 'A . . . at high tide an underwater passageway opens up. I swam out.'

'Were you given any help?'

'By whom?'

Paschuk rubbed the muzzle of his revolver against his knee, a strangely hypnotic gesture. Polishing before the kill, thought Darcie with a shudder. It was like being circled by a shark. 'Did one of my men let you go?'

He didn't believe her story. He thought it more likely that he had a traitor on his side. Darcie wondered if she could use this to her advantage, but it was hard to think quickly with a gun pointing at you.

'What do you mean?' Darcie picked at some mud on the back of her hand, fearing if she let him see her eyes, he'd guess too much.

'Grudnov has not reported in. Was he the one who helped you?' Paschuk eased off the desk and moved a step nearer.

Grudnov? Could that be the man who fell over her earlier on the steps to the beach? What should she say?

Attacking suddenly, Paschuk lunged forward and grabbed the front of her shirt. He lifted her to her feet and shook her. 'Look at me, girl! Is he behind this?'

'Let her go!' shouted Jake.

Paschuk ignored him and tightened his grip. 'I have suspected for some time that I have a traitor in my camp. Is Grudnov a Russian agent?'

'I . . . I don't know what you're talking about,' Darcie gasped.

Carmen put her arms around Darcie from behind and wrapped her fingers around Paschuk's wrist. 'General, that is enough!'

Paschuk let go of Darcie. She fell backwards on to Carmen, sending them sprawling on the sofa.

'It is not enough, Madam Secretary General. She knows more than she is saying and I'm going to get it out of her.' He swung the gun to point at Jake's foot. 'Answer me or I will put a bullet in your friend.'

Darcie met Jake's panicked gaze. 'I . . . I'm not sure, General. I did swim out – I really did. No one helped me. I don't know anyone called Grudnov.'

Bang!

Darcie flinched, eyes closed. When she opened them, she saw the bullet had ploughed into the rug by Jake's toes. He was staring at his shoe, in disbelief that his foot was still in one piece.

'I swear I'm telling you the truth!' Her voice cracked.

As the words left her lips, there came three enormous flash-bangs in rapid succession. All four threw themselves to the floor as the windows rattled ominously in their frames. Jake and Darcie cracked heads as they each tried to protect the other.

Paschuk rolled over to face the door, swearing in Russian. Two of his men burst in, backs to the room, firing into the corridor. Paschuk made a grab for the nearest hostage – Carmen – and clamped the gun to her forehead, shouting all the while to his soldiers. The two men seized Darcie and Jake, weapons digging into their ribs as they pulled them from the floor.

Ears still ringing, Darcie had difficulty making out what was happening outside the room. She heard the staccato burst of gunfire, boots, then silence.

It was broken by a voice on a crackling loud-speaker. 'General Paschuk, come out with your hands above your head!' Though distorted, Darcie thought she recognized the voice. It was Captain Mahoney – Midge – commander of Stingo's SAS squad.

'*Nyet!*' Paschuk shouted into the hall. 'We have three hostages, including the secretary general. If you make a move, they will die with us. We have the place filled with explosives – one move and I blow us all up.' He prodded Carmen with the gun. 'Tell them I am serious, Secretary General.'

Carmen cleared her throat, her voice commend-ably steady. 'He is holding me and two children. I believe he is serious about his threat to use violence.'

A pause. 'State your demands, General.'

'A helicopter with plenty of fuel. Land it on the lawn then leave it empty. I want my men freed. No tricks.' He turned Carmen to face Darcie. 'If it is not here by 0700, I shoot the girl. Tell your superiors that negotiations are relocating to Tazbekistan.'

Midge, the stocky silver-haired leader of the SAS squad, contacted headquarters using his secure satellite line.

'All but three of the hostages successfully extracted from location,' he reported. 'Basement and main hall under our control.'

'But?' prompted Gladys Smith, her eyes fixed on the video images of the recent assault replaying on the screen in front of her – a flash, the entry of a squad of black-clad men, a pause, then streams of confused hostages being evacuated via the kitchens as planned.

'Paschuk had taken the secretary general, Darcie and a boy into another room for questioning so they were not present for the initial assault. Foreign Secretary Riddell says that Darcie is injured.' Midge glanced over to Riddell, Turgenov and Deputy Mila, all of whom had insisted on remaining behind to aid with negotiations. They were sitting together on a bench, looking grey with tiredness, the men's bow ties askew. Riddell was chewing nervously on a stick of gum; Turgenov helping himself to a fortifying glass of brandy; only Mila sat still, eyes closed as she contemplated the horror of her countryman's actions. Her horrid pink dress undulated in the breeze from the open doorways like a sea anemone.

'Paschuk is demanding a helicopter,' Midge continued. 'If he doesn't get it, he's going to kill Darcie.'

Stingo swore – he'd thought she'd be safe by now, thought he could breathe easily for the first time in hours.

Mrs Smith barely flinched. 'Options?'

Stingo was already on the phone making arrangements for the helicopter. Though worried out of his mind for Darcie, he was too professional to let that stop him doing his job.

Midge pinched the bridge of his nose, thinking fast. 'Breaking into that room without causing the death of one or more of the hostages would be nearly impossible, ma'am. If we try and smoke them out, I judge that Paschuk will carry out his threat. He only needs the secretary general; the two young people are expendable.'

As he finished speaking, his colleague, Knife, came in holding a fair-haired boy by the scruff of the neck.

'Found this in the rifle range,' Knife explained, shoving Hugo towards a bench.

Midge gave a grim smile; he and his men had no love for the boy who had given Darcie such grief in Nairobi.

'Found something of yours, ma'am,' Midge told HQ.

'Put Hugo on the line,' ordered Mrs Smith. 'Hugo, what is Darcie's condition?'

'Last I saw Darcie, she was jumping on cars,' Hugo replied. 'I'd say she was OK unless that meathead did something when he caught her. She did have a crack on the temple when she swam out of the cell we were trapped in, but I don't think it was serious.'

'The hostages said she collapsed under questioning from Paschuk.'

Hugo shrugged. 'What else could she do? Tell him to expect the rescue party? Let him shoot her?'

'My thought exactly. So we'll assume she is well enough to be thinking straight. Put Captain Mahoney back on.'

Midge took the phone. 'Our orders?'

'We'll give Paschuk his helicopter as he asked, but we'll make it a slow one. I assume he intends to fly out of St Helen's to rejoin his aircraft at Bristol

Airport. Cover the exit but make sure you get your team to Bristol before he arrives. We'll look for an opportunity to take him on transfer to the plane. But you have authorisation from the prime minister to go in hard at the first sign that he is going to harm the hostages.'

'Yes, ma'am.'

'Oh, and Captain?'

'Yes, ma'am?'

'Keep Hugo with you – he might prove useful.'

12

Darcie had been tied back-to-back with Jake and left in a corner at the foot of the sofa. They were holding hands, drawing comfort from being with each other.

'You all right?' whispered Jake.

'I'm OK.' Darcie squeezed his fingers.

'We could do with that bodyguard friend of yours right now, couldn't we?'

Darcie almost smiled, understanding that this was his way of apologising for what he'd said the night before. 'Yeah, but his mates are outside now – I've worked with them: they're the best.'

'Silence!' roared Paschuk. He turned to the walrus-moustached guard. 'Shoot them if they speak again.'

Carmen had been allowed a chair, her wrists and

feet bound securely. The normally immaculate secretary general looked exhausted, her long black hair tumbling messily over one shoulder, mascara smeared, but somehow she retained her dignity, refusing to show any weakness before their captors. Darcie used the long minutes of waiting to study the guards. The moustached one she remembered from earlier. He had a broad, flat face, burnished to a deep tan, and dark eyes; he reminded her of a fanciful picture she'd once seen of Genghis Khan, so she gave him that nickname in her head. The other guard was tall and lanky with a thin boyish face. The most remarkable thing about him was his pale blue eyes: their expression seemed almost innocent, certainly at odds with the gun he was toting. Darcie guessed he was only a few years older than her.

The silence was broken by Carmen. 'So, General, what mad plan have you come up with now?' she asked acerbically.

Paschuk had found a decanter of brandy and poured himself a glass. He tossed it back as if it were water – the only sign that he was nervous.

'Not mad, Madame Lopez. With you as my guest, I can guarantee a safe return to Jalabad and restraint on the part of the Russians while I strengthen my hold on power.'

'You overestimate my importance, General.'

He waved the decanter towards her, a silent offer. Carmen shook her head.

'I think not. I was wrong to threaten to kill you earlier – my temper got the better of me. I have known all along that you are the . . . how do you say? . . . the trump card. A symbol of the United Nations. Even the Russians will not risk you. No, they will wait and see what I do.'

'And what is that?'

'Declare war on the oppressors.'

Carmen shook her head in disbelief. 'Go to war with Russia! You are mad.'

'No, determined. You forget Tazbekistan is home to a nuclear weapons base. By now my men should have overcome the Russian troops guarding Goraty and have it under Tazbek control. It will not take long to redirect those missiles from Beijing to Moscow.'

Carmen struggled to find words. What he was describing was so horrific. 'You would destroy Moscow?'

He emptied the decanter. 'If necessary. If the choice is between the survival of my people and that of Russia, I know what I have to do.'

Paschuk showed no sign of remorse, no self-doubt; he acted like a soldier obeying a superior's orders.

Carmen could not contain her frustration. 'What you have to do is sit at the negotiating table and work out a peace treaty with Minister Turgenov!'

'There is no point. My way, I will win; your way, Tazbekistan would lose everything. Do not mistake me for a softhearted idealist like Rosa Mila. I have the courage to take this path and see it through to the end.'

Carmen laughed, a mocking sound. 'No, I won't confuse the two of you. One is intelligent and brave, wanting to make a future for her people; the other is a deluded coward, hiding behind women and children.' She cast a derisive glance at the guards, hoping they could understand this exchange.

General Paschuk slammed the glass down on the desk; it cracked in to pieces. 'Be careful, Secretary General. If you continue to irritate me, I'm afraid I will have to silence you.'

Carmen tossed her head. 'Kill me and you destroy your chance of escape.'

He flashed her a mean smile, all teeth and no humour. 'I know you better than that. No, it is your little friends who will suffer, not you.'

Carmen glanced across at Darcie and Jake.

'I see you understand.'

She said nothing more.

At 06.55, Darcie heard the sound of an approaching helicopter. Paschuk pulled the drapes aside to look out on the lawn. Watching him, she felt a deep loathing for his clipped movements, his soldier's alertness; he seemed to have no room for pity or concern for others, focused solely on his objective. She realised then what made him different from the other military men, from Stingo and his squad: she knew for a certainty that they could never attain this coldness of purpose, disregarding human life in this way.

'Good. It is here,' he announced. 'Time to go. Petya, untie our guests.'

The man Darcie had thought looked like Genghis Khan freed the hostages and hauled them to their feet. Darcie felt the prickle of pins-and-needles running through her cramped legs.

Paschuk gave a mock bow to the entrance. 'Open the door, Secretary General.'

Using Carmen as a shield, Paschuk marched her to the entrance. He barked something to his men, who dragged Jake and Darcie with them, the moustached Petya in charge of Darcie. She felt the steely strength of the guard's arm across her chest, but he was not rough with her, just insistent. On Paschuk's order, they arranged themselves with the men in the middle and the hostages facing outwards – this way, any sniper would have great difficulty getting a clear shot without hitting a hostage.

'We are coming out,' Paschuk boomed into the hall. The strange party shuffled forwards to be met by silence. They were halfway to the main doors when Rosa Mila stepped out of the banqueting chamber, her hands up to show she was unarmed. She was still dressed in her rumpled pink finery, looking oddly like the good witch from The Wizard of Oz.

'General, please reconsider,' she begged. 'You will destroy any chance Tazbekistan has for peace if you do this.'

'Out of my way, woman,' growled Paschuk.

Deputy Mila's hands trembled as she held them aloft. 'Then at least let the children go. Take me instead if you need another hostage.'

Paschuk's answer was to shoot. Mila dived for cover as the plaster just over her head fragmented. Thankfully he had not been aiming to kill.

'I am bored of your whining, Mila. Your services

are no longer required in Tazbekistan.' With that he pushed Carmen through the main doors and out on to the gravel drive.

On the lawn, the military helicopter waited like a broken-winged bird, blades drooping. Being towed backwards, Darcie had a chance to look behind them at the house. She saw a shaken Rosa Mila helped to her feet by John Riddell and the Russian minister, Turgenov. There was no sign of the SAS rescue party, but that was no surprise, as they would not be seen unless they wanted to. She knew from past experience that they would be watching her and the other hostages closely, filming their every move. Terrified though she was for herself, she knew that there was much more at stake now than the safety of three people. They had to know about the general's insane plan to launch a nuclear strike against Moscow. Could she get a message to them? Her guard was occupied scanning the grounds for threats; he was only holding her with one hand as he held his gun in the other. That left her right hand free. She brought it up to her chest and made a gesture with her index finger indicating a missile taking off, followed by sketching an M on her stomach. She repeated the signal three times, hoping that someone would guess correctly and not think she had chosen a bizarre moment to be rude.

'Where are my men?' roared Paschuk as they reached the cover of the helicopter.

Out of the main doors of St Helen's ran seven newly released Tazbeks from Paschuk's delegation. Though their weapons had been confiscated, they surrounded their general, protecting him with their bodies like a ball in a rugby scrum as he climbed into the helicopter. The hostages were pushed in after him and the door slammed shut. The general himself sat at the controls, cracking his knuckles as he worked out the unfamiliar layout.

'Time to go home,' he announced.

MI6 Headquarters, Vauxhall, London: cool and cloudy,
13°C

Gladys Smith ran the video of the takeoff again and again.

'What is she doing?' she asked.

Stingo rubbed a hand wearily across his eyes. It had been a long night and Darcie was still in danger.

He wished he could have ordered her out of there hours ago, but the politicians had had other ideas. He cursed Christopher Lock silently. 'I dunno. The second gesture looks like an "M."'

'Get her father in here. Maybe he will know.'

Stingo found Michael Lock in the coffee lounge of the MI6 building. He was standing with his back to the room, staring down on the Thames. In the pale dawn light, the river looked grey and chill, flecked with leaves from the trees shedding along the embankment. The tide moved at a rapid clip against the supports of Vauxhall Bridge, giving the unnerving sensation that the world was on fast-forward.

'Michael, we need your help,' Stingo said, putting a hand on his arm.

Darcie's father visibly pulled himself together, squaring his shoulders and holding up his head. 'Of course.'

'She'll be all right. She's been in worse scrapes than this. I've seen her face impossible odds and beat them.'

Michael gave a mirthless laugh. 'Stingo, the last six months have been hell on earth. I have lost count of the number of times my daughter's life has been in danger.'

'I know,' said Stingo quietly.

'When we get her back, I am going to resign and take her somewhere very quiet and very boring.'

Stingo laughed as Michael wanted, though he thought this good news indeed if Darcie's father was serious. He had had enough of worrying about what was happening to Darcie Lock, what mad killer would harm her next. The girl deserved a break.

'Does Ginnie know what's happening?' Stingo asked as he guided Michael to the command centre.

Michael held out open hands in a gesture of despair. 'I don't know. She's out of contact. Darcie's name hasn't been made public, but the Americans must realise by now who is with the secretary general. Will they tell her or not? I've no idea. She might guess, I suppose, if she catches the news.'

Mrs Smith looked up as they entered. 'Ah, Michael, I'm glad you're here. Can you take a look at this please?'

Michael examined the footage, brow creased. He turned to Stingo. 'She looks unharmed, doesn't she – despite the cut, I mean?'

Stingo nodded. 'Yeah, she seems fine.'

Mrs Smith tapped Michael's shoulder. 'What do you think she's trying to tell us? We need an answer.

The helicopter is due to touch down in Bristol in the next hour.'

Michael paused the video as Darcie jabbed upwards. 'The other sign is an "M", but this I don't understand. What has she heard that she's trying to pass on?'

'It's crude – looks like some kind of upward movement,' suggested Stingo.

'How would you signal a plane taking off, Michael?' Mrs Smith took a step away from the screen, her brow furrowed in thought.

Michael mimicked his daughter, holding his arm across his chest. 'I think I'd make the wings – finger and thumb spread. Helicopter, I'd do a circle.'

'A rocket – a missile.' Stingo tapped the image on the screen. 'Yeah, it's some kind of missile.'

'Missile to "M",' murmured Mrs Smith.

'Or "M" stands for missile?' suggested Michael.

Mrs Smith shook her head. 'I hope I'm wrong but I think she means Paschuk's planning to launch an attack on Moscow.'

The pieces of the puzzle were tumbling into place with frightening speed.

'Goraty,' said Stingo.

'The nuclear base,' added Michael. 'It has five SS-18s; each of those missiles has ten separately targeted warheads. The damage he could do is unimaginable. We have to tell the Russians.'

Mrs Smith frowned. 'They probably already know. The coup has been running for twelve hours now – the base would have been a priority for both sides. Still, get on the phone to the Russian embassy, Michael.'

Stingo was still staring at the screen, eyes fixed on Darcie. 'Permission to rejoin my squad, ma'am?'

His request took Mrs Smith by surprise. 'What? Why?'

'If they don't free the hostages in Bristol, then this little party is going to Tazbekistan and I want to be there. I'm the squad's Russian speaker for a start. And if Darcie's heading into a nuclear confrontation, she sure as hell shouldn't be on her own.'

Mrs Smith checked the radar display showing the location of the helicopter and gave a curt nod. 'All right. Get yourself to your squad. I'll tell Captain Mahoney to expect you and get them to go slow on the refuelling of the Tazbek jet – that should buy you some time.'

Darcie and Jake sat side-by-side on the floor of the helicopter. The vibrations from the engine were so intense that Darcie felt her teeth rattle and her thighs were numbed by contact with the metal-plated floor. She didn't envy Carmen her padded seat up in the cockpit, however, as she had to endure Paschuk's company. In the cargo hold of the helicopter, their guards seemed happy to ignore the two youngsters during the lull in the fighting.

'Darcie?' Jake whispered.

'Yes?'

'What's going to happen to us?'

Petya, the Genghis Khan lookalike, glanced over at them but made no move to stop them talking. No way could he have heard with all the noise from the engines but still Darcie had noticed that he was the only terrorist who paid them any attention.

Darcie dropped her head forward to hide the fact that she was replying. 'I don't know. But there are good people looking for us right now. They'll come up with something, I'm sure of it. We just need to . . .' she was going to say 'stay alive' but decided this sounded too alarming, '. . . not panic.'

Jake slipped his arm around her and pulled so she could rest her head on his shoulder. 'You're amazing. Without you, I'd be a wreck.'

Darcie allowed herself to sag against him. 'Well, it's not exactly the first time for me.'

Jake chuckled, then rubbed a grimy hand over his face. Both of them were exhausted. 'Darcie Galt, you're good to have around. Do you, like, want to go out with me when this madness is over?' He began to laugh – it was either that or cry. 'I've got great timing, haven't I?'

'The best. As long as it doesn't involve gunmen and deranged generals, then yeah, OK.'

'I think I can promise that.'

'That's settled then.' Darcie snuggled against him, letting his presence calm her. She'd been in frightening situations before but never with someone on her side. Drifting off to sleep, she realised that, despite everything, she could still find things to be thankful for.

The helicopter circled the runway at Bristol airport and then put down close to the Tazbeks' 747. At the wing of the plane, a fuel lorry was still at work. Jake gently shook Darcie awake as the engines whined down.

'Time to rock and roll, sister,' he said in a low voice.

Carmen entered the cargo bay with Paschuk. Her eyes immediately flicked to Jake and Darcie, relieved to see that they were unharmed. Paschuk was giving orders to his men in Russian, but it was evident from the mounting tension that they all understood that this was the most dangerous part of the operation. Finally he turned to his hostages.

'Madam Secretary General, you must part with one of your little friends as I need them to create a diversion to get us away without problems. I have decided that we will leave the girl behind. She proved capable of making much trouble for us. I do not want her along on the next part of our journey. Say goodbye.'

Darcie was stunned. Leave her behind? A diversion? None of that sounded good, not when he knew she'd overheard much of their plans. Her grip on Jake's hand tightened.

Carmen didn't understand – she thought Paschuk was doing her a favour.

'Thank you, General, but why not release the boy as well, while you have the chance? You only need me.'

Paschuk shook his head. 'I need your cooperation and for that I need the boy. We leave now.' He turned his eyes to Petya. 'Make it look good,' he ordered in Russian.

The guard shouldered his rifle and gave a curt nod.

Carmen swooped down on Darcie and planted a

kiss on her cheek. She had tears in her eyes. 'I'm pleased you're out of this, my dear.'

Jake was pulled away from Darcie with more reluctance. 'I'll see you for that date, remember?' he said hoarsely. 'It's a done deal.'

Darcie could only manage a nod as she watched them being hustled from the helicopter and over the short stretch of tarmac towards the steps up to the plane.

13

Bristol Airport, England: bright spells, 15°C

Over in the long grass by the edge of the runway, his men arranged in a semi-circle around the 747, SAS Commander Mahoney was waiting for the signal to go. The helicopter had put down in an awkward spot, half-hidden by the fuselage of the jet.

'Two hostages, the boy and Madame Lopez, Paschuk and one other terrorist in sight, ma'am,' Midge reported. 'No sign of Zebra as yet.' A bead of sweat trickled down his brow. They had only ten seconds max while the terrorists were out in the open, but to move now would leave Darcie at the mercy of the men in the helicopter. They'd been planning to target that once the hostages were clear but now plans had to change. 'Do we have the green light, over?'

In the command centre, Mrs Smith watched the real-time images of the four people moving across the tarmac. They were getting too close – the small window of opportunity was passing. She would have to risk Darcie to save the others. Clearing her throat, she was about to give the order when the door on the far side of the helicopter opened and Darcie was pushed out, followed by a gunman. The SAS team would not have a clear sight of them from their position.

'Captain, third hostage at rear door far side of helicopter. At least one gunman with her. Over.' Paschuk and his party were close to the steps.

'Roger that. Are we good to go, over?' Midge asked with an edge of desperation.

Mrs Smith watched in horror as the gunman made Darcie kneel on the tarmac with her hands behind her head, words momentarily failing her. He was going to execute her.

'Negative, Captain. Take out the man holding Darcie.'

In that short space of deliberation, Paschuk

reached the steps and disappeared inside the plane. Mrs Smith cursed, already wondering if she'd made the wrong call.

Knees jabbed by grit on the concrete, Darcie could feel a shiver run between her shoulder blades. She could sense everything in crystal clear detail: the heady scent of aviation fuel, the cold light breeze toying with her hair, and the presence of Petya behind her, so square and uncompromising, his face giving away nothing. The flat, featureless space of the airfield stretched out on all sides, no sign of help anywhere to be seen.

'You don't have to do this,' she said desperately. She felt numb, frozen, terror darkening her mind; it was like drowning in deep water under thick ice.

His answer was to shift and aim the semi-automatic rifle.

'Please!'

'Fall when I shoot,' he said in guttural English.

'What?'

'I do not kill children. Fall when I shoot.'

A lifeline or a cruel lie to make her stay still? Closing her eyes, Darcie waited for the signal.

.   .   .

'Do you have the shot?' Midge asked his sniper, Knife, lying on his stomach ten metres away.

'Negative, sir.'

Shielded by the bulk of the helicopter, Darcie and her captor were out of their reach without the SAS team breaking cover.

'Knife, Merlin: you're with me. Go!' Midge was already up and running, heading away from the plane and around the helicopter, followed by two of his squad. But it was too late. A single shot rang out and Darcie crumpled forward. The terrorist jumped back into the helicopter, taking cover as he opened fire on the three soldiers sprinting towards him. Midge took a bullet in the leg and went down. Knife and Merlin scooped him up under the arms and dragged him to the cover of the fuel lorry, still shooting as they went.

'Two men down,' Knife panted into his helmet microphone.

The rest of the SAS squad pinned the remaining Tazbeks in the helicopter. The situation was rapidly turning into a stalemate.

And out on the tarmac Darcie lay, bullets whistling overhead, pinging off the fuselage. Amazed to be undamaged so far, her greatest fear was being injured in the crossfire. She wondered if she should run for cover but before she could put her thoughts into action, she heard a loud oath from overhead, felt someone grab her jacket and haul her into the shelter of the helicopter.

'You died, remember!' hissed Petya, his breath sour in her face.

Understanding that he intended her to play dead, Darcie slumped against him.

'Why did you get her?' asked one of the other Tazbeks in Russian as he grappled with a new clip of ammunition.

Petya patted Darcie nonchalantly on the back. 'Human shield, Manet. The British won't want me to leave now I've killed their girl but they won't shoot me if I've got her. They can't be certain she's dead.'

'They don't want any of us to leave,' replied the man, returning to his post.

Mrs Smith stared in sick horror at the pictures. She'd lost agents before but never one so young. A teenager. What had she been thinking allowing Darcie to face this level of danger? Her guilt was intensified by Michael Lock's desperate sobs from the other side of the room. She wanted to comfort him but had to stick to her post.

'Message from the control tower, ma'am,' her aide said respectfully. 'Paschuk is threatening to kill the boy if his men are not allowed to reach the plane. He asks if you require any more proof that he is serious in his threats.'

Mrs Smith dragged the words up like lead weights. 'No proof. Tell the SAS to stand down. We can do no more here.' We could hardly do worse, she added tacitly.

The order was relayed and the guns fell silent.

Darcie lay on the floor of the helicopter, confused by the fact that she was still alive and wondering what she should do now. An order crackled in over the radio and the Tazbeks started to line up by the front exit. At the prompting of his compatriots, Petya reluctantly hauled Darcie over his shoulder. They seemed to be making some black joke out of her presence. He joined the end of the queue to board the plane. As the men jogged over the tarmac, Darcie was able to take a quick look at their surroundings through her dangling hair. The fuel lorry disengaged from the wing and trundled away. Three soldiers retreated in the distance, the two on the outside supporting the man in the middle as his leg dragged behind. Petya began to mount the stairs. He couldn't mean to take her in the plane, could he? Darcie braced herself, expecting to be dumped on the top step, but instead he took her inside and walked quickly through the passenger cabin to reach the storage area at the back of the 747. Pushing open the concertina door of a wardrobe full of uniforms, he dropped her to the floor and urged her inside.

'You are dead,' he repeated. 'The general must not know I disobeyed him. I get you when we arrive in Jalabad.'

Snapping the door closed, he left her.

Head still spinning, Darcie wormed her way to the back of the wardrobe, hiding her presence under a greatcoat that had fallen from its hanger. She couldn't understand why Petya had bothered to save her only to bring her on board. He was going to extraordinary lengths to protect both her and the secret of his insubordination. She drew hope from that thought as the engines growled in to life and the plane began its bumpy journey down the runway.

The crisis meeting room fell silent as the men watched the footage of the plane taking off from Bristol. The prime minister swore.

'What a fiasco,' muttered the defence minister.

Christopher Lock had not recovered from watching his granddaughter's execution live on the screen. Everyone was avoiding meeting his eye; it was as if he had become invisible. His knuckles were white as he gripped his briefing papers, scrunching them into a ball.

'The foreign secretary is on the line, Prime Minister,' announced an aide.

The man at the head of the table took the call. 'John, did you see all that?'

'Yes, Prime Minister,' a crackly voice replied on the line. 'But Minister Turgenov's with me and he has something he wishes to tell us. That guard – the one who shot Darcie – well, Turgenov thinks that he didn't.'

'What!'

Christopher felt his heart clench; he wondered for a panicked moment if he was having a heart attack. Hope almost felt worse than grief. He took a gulp of water and dug deep for control.

'He's their man – the Russians, I mean,' continued Riddell. 'He is under orders to stay by Paschuk at all costs but it appears that this was one demand on him that he could not carry out. There's every chance the girl's still alive.'

The prime minister gave a sign to the technicians to run the footage again. 'We'll get our analysts on it, John, right away. Why the hell didn't he tip us off about the hostage taking then?'

'Apparently he did, via the Russian intelligence services, but I don't think even their man realised how far General Paschuk was prepared to go. SIS passed the warning on to us but it appeared . . . er . . . too late to call off the conference at the time.'

'But does Turgenov know why his agent took the girl on board?'

'He believes that his man didn't have a choice. The agent opted to bring Darcie out of the crossfire – at his own peril I might add – but he couldn't let her get up and walk away in front of the Tazbeks or the television cameras – that would have entirely blown his cover with Paschuk.'

'What will he do with her now?'

'Hand her over to his Russian handlers in Jalabad – when and if he can slip her away that is. He has to think of his mission first; I'm afraid the girl is only of secondary importance bearing in mind what is at stake here.'

After several calming breaths, Christopher had recovered sufficiently from his shock to contribute to the discussion. Of course, his granddaughter wasn't dead; she couldn't be.

'You know what that means, Prime Minister?' Lock said, carefully straightening his papers.

'No, Christopher, what does it mean?'

'It means that we've got our own agent on the inside – one that Paschuk thinks is dead.'

The flight seemed endless to Darcie, cooped up in the wardrobe. She had been left alone in a strange windowless limbo where she had no sense of time. Days could have gone by – though she suspected it was only one – and she would not have known. Darcie dozed fitfully until the aircraft began its descent. For the past few hours she had been trying to ignore the fact that she needed the bathroom.

Spies in Hollywood blockbusters never seemed to have that problem, she thought miserably, despite all the drinks they had in swish bars.

A clunk reverberated through the wardrobe as the landing gear was engaged. She braced herself across the width of the wardrobe and covered her head with her arms. Having been so grateful to be alive, it was only now that she wondered what waited outside. A country in the midst of a war – and she spoke not a word of the local languages. If Petya abandoned her now, she would be in serious trouble.

Who was she kidding? She already was in serious trouble.

The plane touched down, the engines thrown in reverse thrust as momentum slowed. Welcome to Tazbekistan.

Jalabad Airport, Tazbekistan: Slow-moving high pressure system, 25°C

The plane was empty. Paschuk and the two hostages had left amidst much noise and confusion, roaring away in a fleet of army trucks. Darcie waited in the wardrobe, her knuckles white as she held her fists clenched on her bent knees. What next? Now Petya had got her this far alive, was she on her own? Did she dare risk leaving?

Outside she heard a clatter on the steps – Darcie tensed, ready to make a dash for it if someone discovered her. Then the whine of a vacuum cleaner cut through the silence, an absurdly ordinary sound. The country was in the midst of a civil war but some cleaning lady was still going to do her job. Darcie almost smiled, until she realised that a conscientious cleaner was far more of a danger to her than the less inquisitive soldiers that surrounded Paschuk. She debated if she could just get up and walk out, pretending she was supposed to be here. Dressed in bedraggled combat trousers and St Helen's T-shirt, she doubted she'd blend in with the locals. Or would she? Her clothes were pretty universal for kids her age, weren't they? Unless this was one of those Central Asian countries with a strict dress code for girls . . . She wracked her memory trying to recall everything she had heard about Tazbekistan and came away with a zero. But they'd had a woman as leader – Deputy Mila – and she'd worn a suit – that suggested a certain amount of freedom for girls so perhaps she would not be too conspicuous if she ventured outside? Taking the chance was surely better than being caught cowering in a wardrobe.

And to be honest she had to find a bathroom and quickly or this would all become a whole lot worse.

Mind made up, Darcie pulled herself to her feet. Her limbs tingled with pins and needles, protesting at having spent so long in that cramped cubbyhole.

Grabbing an empty flight bag from the overhead shelf, she slid the door aside and stepped out into the cabin. The mosquito sound of the vacuum cleaner continued unabated in the first class lounge.

Act as if you're supposed to be here, Darcie told herself as she steeled herself to walk confidently towards the exit at the front of the plane. She caught a glimpse of the bobbing rear end of a woman in a blue nylon uniform as she swung the vacuum cleaner between the seats. If her luck held, the woman would not even notice her departure. Darcie strode swiftly to the door to take her first breath of Tazbek air.

And immediately took a step back. A guard stood at the bottom of the steps, facing away from the aircraft, casually smoking a cigarette. Tazbeks obviously hadn't heard about lung cancer or the perils of mixing fire with aviation fuel. There was no way she was going to get past without being seen and now she was stuck between him and the cleaner. In those few seconds of hesitation, the noise of the vacuum cleaner died and a woman called out a challenge from the depths of the plane. That was enough to attract the attention of the guard. He turned around, gun cradled in his arms – and smiled.

It was Petya. Darcie's heart flipped in relief. The

cleaner appeared at Darcie's side and poked her in the ribs, chattering away in Russian, but Darcie had no trouble translating it as 'what the devil do you think you're doing here?' Coming to her rescue, Petya strode up the steps as he answered on Darcie's behalf. Without waiting to pause for a breath, he grabbed her arm and towed her after him. As they clattered down the steps, he took the empty flight bag and waved it at the woman as if exhibiting the evidence.

'What did you say?' Darcie muttered as they walked briskly off across the airfield. Petya walked with the muscle-bound gait of a boxer. Despite his very different looks, he reminded Darcie a little of the SAS guys she knew; she suspected he would have fitted right in with the squad under different circumstances – though he might have to lose the disconcerting moustache first if he wanted to escape a ribbing.

'I told her you were my daughter. I said I had sent you in to fetch something I had forgotten.' Petya gave a hoarse laugh and then ruffled Darcie's black hair – whether as a friendly gesture or for the benefit of the watching cleaner, she wasn't sure. Perhaps both. 'Lucky for us that you are not blonde. You could be Tazbek girl.'

'I can't believe we got away with that.' Darcie shook her head in bewilderment. Everything was happening too quickly. Who would've thought last week that she'd be in the middle of Asia now, walking in the hot sun across an airport runway, a line of blue hills on the horizon like a row of shark's teeth. Everything looked weirdly peaceful considering the country was at war.

'We have not got out yet.' Petya's expression left her in no doubt they were not safe. 'I will take you somewhere you can hide, but then I must leave you. I have a job to do.'

Darcie did not like the sound of being left, but knew she had no choice. She owed a serious debt to this man and was not about to make his life any more difficult. Whatever his motivations for saving her, she did not want him regretting his merciful impulse. Approaching the terminal building, Petya pushed open a pair of cracked glass doors and they walked into the tomb-like customs hall unchallenged. The baggage conveyor belts were stilled, an unclaimed parcel spilling its contents over the edge like road kill. With no international flights coming in and the Tazbek army in occupation, the airport staff were keeping their heads down. If they were there at all, they were not visible. That made the

246 / JULIA GOLDING

presence of the cleaning lady on the aircraft even more odd.

After a brief pit stop in the washroom, they continued through the terminal buildings.

'Why did that woman come out to clean the plane?' Darcie whispered as Petya led her past the empty duty-free shops.

'Money,' he explained in clear but heavily accented English. 'She was looking for stuff she could sell – magazines, alcohol, cigarettes. It is a perk of her job. She thought you were after the same thing – that is why she was cross.' Petya pushed his way through a door marked with a big red sign that could only mean 'no entry'. 'I was waiting for her to finish before coming in to get you.'

'I thought she'd find me if I stayed where I was.'

He nodded. 'You are probably right. Your way was better. I doubt she will report seeing you.'

'But she might.'

He shrugged, a gesture to say that there was nothing either of them could do about it.

'What did you tell the general? Where's he gone?'

'I told him the truth.' Petya grinned again, displaying his tobacco-stained front teeth. 'I told him I had to dispose of you. As to where he has gone, that is none of your business now. You are out of this.'

'My friends – are they safe?'

Petya said nothing, which was as good as a 'no'. 'Come. I only have a few hours before I am missed.'

In the parking lot outside, there were no cars to be seen, just the white lines marking out the bays in a cracked concrete desert.

'Where is everyone?' Darcie wondered aloud.

'The airport is an important target,' Petya explained. 'Most people are staying far away in case the Russians decide to bomb the runway.'

Darcie took an anxious look up at the pale blue skies. They were empty of all but wispy white clouds and a skein of swallows unravelling in loops across the blank canvas. But it wouldn't take long for a MiG jet to scream into view like a knife slash across the peaceful picture.

Anxious to get to somewhere considerably safer, she asked, 'So how do we get away from here?'

Petya shouldered his gun. 'We walk.' He unwound the chequered scarf knotted around his throat and tossed it to her. 'Put this over your head.'

She followed his order. 'Do women have to cover up in Tazbekistan then? I'm sorry I don't know much about your culture – I feel completely stupid.'

Petya tweaked the scarf so it covered the back of her neck, his moustache twitching. 'We are a moderate country. We have Muslims, Buddhists and Christians living side-by-side. Some wear the veil but it is not required.'

'So why do I need the scarf?'

He nodded to the sky. 'It is hot – and we don't want you recognised.'

Good point. Darcie threw the end over her shoulder so that her mouth and nose were hidden by a fold of cloth.

'I'm ready. Let's go.'

They had not gone far down the road back to the capital when they met the first roadblock. A row of green-clad soldiers stood guarding a spiked barrier. This must have come as no surprise to Petya for he did not slow.

'It will be all right,' he said softly, noticing her hesitation. 'They know me. Do not speak.' He fumbled in his pocket and brought out a packet of the ubiquitous cigarettes and lit one for himself. He approached the soldiers as if on a Sunday stroll. Darcie dropped a pace behind and kept her eyes on the scuffed toes of her trainers. Petya called out a greeting to the men and stopped to offer them the cigarettes.

Imagining how Petya's real daughter would behave, Darcie stood to one side as if bored, shredding a piece of the tough grass plucked from the verge. The men exchanged a few words and handed round the packet, then they stood back to let the pair through. One called out something as they passed, making the others laugh. Petya answered, clapping Darcie on the back.

'What did he say?' she asked once they were out of sight.

'He asked me to bear him in mind when it came to arranging your marriage.' He chuckled at her shocked expression. 'He was just being nice – it was his way of thanking me for the cigarettes. It means nothing.'

They walked for a mile or so in silence, both deep in their separate thoughts. Though knowing from experience that she could trust him, Darcie tried to work out why Petya was going to these lengths to protect her. If she could only understand him, she felt she would have a better chance of emerging from this situation unscathed. He'd been prepared to go against his master for her, which didn't tally with the fanatical devotion shown by the other men. They had been prepared to protect Paschuk with their bodies when they had no weapons; from everything she'd seen, Petya lacked this intense loyalty to the general.

Reaching the outskirts of the capital, they passed a tangle of wild apple trees – the year's crop dropping to the ground, smashed red baubles smelling of cider. Set back from the road straggled a row of pale-brick cottages with ill-kempt gardens. In the rough verge a goat stood tethered to a post. It bleated a challenge, its devil-eyed stare a threat. It had mown the grass in a perfect circle as far as its rope would reach like the crop marks some claimed were made by UFOs. But Darcie was the alien here.

'Why do you support the general?' she asked Petya, trying to make sense of this place and its people.

Petya dug in his pocket and pulled out a canteen of water. He offered it to her, and she took it gratefully. All this walking was making her thirsty.

'It is complicated. I am doing my job, but I do not work for Paschuk.'

Darcie asked the obvious question. 'So who do you work for?'

'I am a loyal citizen.' Seeing her confusion, Petya added: 'You see, Darcie, you have come to a very mixed-up place. We Tazbeks are like dogs arguing over a bone. In my opinion, Tazbek should stay part of Russia – as a province with our own culture and traditions. I do no support the move to break away. It is madness. And I believe it is possible to be both Tazbek and Russian, like your Scots who are both Scottish and British.'

'So you're a . . . a spy for the Russians?'

He held up his hand to silence her. 'That is the last time you should say it aloud. I will hand you over to my contact in the Russian government when it is safe to do so. Until then, you must forget what I have told you and keep out of sight. If you are discovered, my cover is blown and I will have no chance to stop Paschuk.' He paused and turned her so he could look down into her face to reinforce the point. 'You understand how important that is – more important even than the life of a single person?'

Darcie nodded. She had not forgotten Paschuk's threat of nuclear war on Moscow. 'I'll do what you need me to do,' she vowed. 'And thank you for taking the risk.'

'No need to thank me.' With a flash of a smile, he started walking again. 'I am very pleased you are alive. I thought for a moment at the airport that I was going to lose you in the crossfire – I would not have slept easy for many nights if that had happened.'

Darcie resettled the scarf over her face. 'I think you must be a good man. I'll make sure I tell your government so.'

He gave a wry laugh. 'I imagine they are furious at me for risking my position with Paschuk. It took a long time to set that up and now they need me with him. I suppose I am what you would call the last line of defence for Moscow.'

'What does that mean? Have you been ordered to kill him?'

'If there is no other way. I may have to do so with or without orders to stop him using nuclear weapons – that has been left to my discretion. But I still hope that this coup will crumble and he will be tried for war crimes.' He spat at the hot tarmac. 'To think I once admired him for his convictions, even if I thought him wrong! The hostage taking was a stupid risk, losing him any potential support from other governments in the region. No, he will fail. A long spell in a maximum-security prison is what he deserves and I would like to be the man to put him there.'

They passed through a second roadblock without incident. A rusting iron bridge took them over a sluggish river. In the chasm below, the brown water trickled between boulders stained with oil. Darcie didn't like the look of the yellow scum gathering along the shore and hoped this was not the source of her drinking water while in Jalabad. Once beyond the river, normal life resumed: the broad, tree-lined boulevards of the Tazbek capital were jammed with cars, lorries and horse-drawn carts. After the silence of the airport road, Darcie felt as if the mute button had suddenly been switched off. The noise was immense: people shouting, cars revving, power tools gunning away on a building site. The air smelled of diesel and dust. Roadside markets were doing a bustling trade; country women in flowered dresses and bright cotton head-scarves sat in front of baskets of dried apricots, tangerines, pomegranates, and buckets of live fish – the latter would at intervals be pulled out, bashed with a stone, then wrapped in newspaper for a customer. It gave a whole new meaning to the word 'fresh'. Nothing was as Darcie expected for a country in crisis.

'Where's the war?' she asked in confusion.

'For the moment, in the north of the city,' Petya explained, cupping his hand around her ear to speak over the noise. 'Until it reaches here, life continues. Now we must not speak again. Too many people.'

Darcie nodded and followed him over to a taxi parked in front of a wayside teashop. The driver was sitting in the shade of an elm tree, sipping from a little white cup that he had just refilled from a gleaming silver samovar. From the even more extravagant size of his moustache, Darcie realised Petya was not alone in his hair-styling preferences. Behind the taxi driver stood an empty marble plinth, its edge chipped but the hammer-and-sickle inscription still legible. Darcie had the impression that the bronze Lenin, who had once dominated the square, haranguing the people from his pedestal, had wandered off in disgust now no one was paying him attention.

After a brief bit of haggling with Petya, the driver drained the golden liquid, threw some coins on the table, and ushered them over to his car.

As the taxi edged its way through the traffic, Darcie wondered why Petya was taking such a public route in her company. In Nairobi, Mrs Smith had told her about the psychology of what she called 'hiding in plain sight': people did not notice if you did not look as if you had anything to hide. This must be the tack Petya had chosen, but still it was undoubtedly a risk. What if Paschuk became suspicious and asked the men at the roadblocks what Petya had done with her body? He would be furious to learn she walked off the plane rather than been buried in a shallow grave somewhere on the airfield. She had to hope that the general would be too busy to check what had become of her.

The taxi drew up outside a low-rise apartment building in a quiet side street. Petya handed the driver some money, exchanged a few friendly remarks, then joined Darcie on the pavement to watch the car depart. He didn't enter the nearest building but instead retraced their route to the corner. Crossing the road, he led her through an archway into another apartment block, across a courtyard full of cars and up a flight of external stairs to a balcony running along the first floor. The building looked ancient. The balustrade was beautifully decorated with a carved wooden lattice and the doorways decorated with plaster friezes of fruits and flowers. Cracks ran crazily across the walls, memorials to past earthquakes. From the communal layout of the courtyard, Darcie guessed it had once been the home of one rich family, now divided to house many.

Petya entered a door halfway down the landing without knocking, calling out as he went in. A woman answered from inside, sounding surprised and relieved. Darcie lingered in the entry as he disappeared into a room off the corridor. She admired the crimson and blue tasselled cloth that framed the doorway and the collection of horse-whips, quivers and bridle bells displayed on the wall, fragments of the culture Petya had mentioned. Gently touching a brass bell, it rang with a husky note. In the distance, she could hear Petya reassuring the woman – his wife? – and then murmuring an explanation. Darcie grimaced as she imagined the conversation: yes, I'm fine but I've decided to put us all in danger by parking an English girl here. No, no, the general doesn't know about her and thinks she's dead, but hey, don't worry about that now, I've got to prevent nuclear war.

After only a few moments, Petya returned, his arm around a small, elfin woman with short dark hair.

'Darcie, this is my wife, Leila. She will look after you.'

The woman held out a birdlike hand to pat Darcie's wrist, her eyes glistening as she chattered away in Russian. She was working hard not to show how terrified she was by this development. Darcie had never felt more awkward.

'I'm sorry to put you to this trouble,' she replied, even though Leila could not understand her.

'No trouble,' lied Petya. 'Let me introduce you to Babushka – our grandmother – then I must go.'

He ushered her down the corridor to the door at the far end and knocked loudly before opening it. Darcie blinked as she looked inside. It was another world entirely to the Tazbek decorations of the hall-way. Babushka sat in a chair knitting a red jumper, surrounded by mementoes of the Soviet era: posters of square-jawed workers hauling golden sheaves home to collective farms, pin-ups of past heroes – astronauts and sportsmen of the twentieth century. A framed photo of Lenin, founder of the Soviet Union. A sputnik satellite on a little wooden stand.

Petya leaned over the old lady and spoke in a loud voice explaining the presence of his guest. She nodded and smiled at Darcie, beckoning her closer with a knitting needle. Darcie was now able to see the family resemblance to Petya in the shape and colour of Babushka's dark eyes. A stocky, almost mannish figure, her upper lip had a heavy shadow of facial hair. There was something indestructible about her, like an old stubborn tree refusing to be toppled in the gales. She grabbed Darcie's hand and gave it a firm squeeze.

'Mrs Thatcher,' she said in a scratchy voice. 'Winston Churchill. Strong. Good.'

Darcie smiled and nodded, as seemed appropriate. She reciprocated by pointing to the pictures:

'Lenin, Gagarin,' she said, thanking her lucky stars that she'd taken a course on Russian history the year before.

Babushka was delighted by Darcie's recognition of her heroes. 'Strong. Good,' she repeated, stroking the top of the framed portrait.

'Maria Ilianova is a war veteran. She had many medals,' Petya explained proudly, kissing his grandmother on the cheek. 'Look after each other. I will see you soon.'

Babushka's eyes filled with tears as she watched her grandson go. She clasped her hands and raised them, a kind of victory blessing. 'Good boy,' she said to Darcie. 'Proud.'

Darcie nodded. 'Very good.'

15

Somewhere over Southern Russia

The aircraft radio crackled and Mrs Smith came on air.

'I've good news. Kazakhstan has agreed to let you land in one of their western airfields,' she explained to the SAS squad already en route to Central Asia.

'The Russians?' asked Stingo. He had been put in temporary command when

Midge had been hospitalised with his leg-wound; he was now sitting in the co-pilot's chair, leafing through pages of hastily assembled mission briefing. He'd absorbed every word already, but had to keep himself busy to stop thinking about what might be happening to Darcie.

'They refused permission. It's their war and they don't agree that we have a continuing responsibility to the hostages. Understandably they are concentrating on the nuclear threat rather than freeing the secretary general. The Russian army are planning to take back the palace where Paschuk is holed up with the hostages in their own good time. They take the view we might get in the way.'

Stingo swore.

'But,' continued Mrs Smith, 'I have permission for you to take your team into Jalabad thanks to Deputy Mila. She has agreed that you can enter the country to attempt to free the hostages and has said she'd handle the Russians objections when they came.'

Stingo smiled grimly. He just loved politicians. 'Do the Russians know about this?'

'They will – when you've got into the country. That little manoeuvre will be thanks to the Americans who agree with us that it is worth making an attempt to free the secretary general even if the odds of success are unfavourable. They've diverted a helicopter from a base in Afghanistan and they will stay in the area to help with extraction. Just don't annoy the Russians while you're there – keep out of their hair. Your orders are to get well clear of the palace before their assault begins.'

Stingo rubbed a hand wearily over his bristling chin. 'This is getting complicated.'

'Indeed. And make sure Hugo stays out of trouble, please. Use him as a source on the kidnappers but I don't want him anywhere near the action, understood?'

Stingo shot a dark look at the teenager lounging in the seat next to Knife. He was asleep, mouth open and snoring loudly.

'Yes, ma'am, I'll keep him safe. Though, as I said, I would've preferred to jettison him at Bristol.' Or at twenty thousand feet over the Black Sea – he wasn't fussy.

'Don't underestimate him – he's good at his job.'

Rather than waste airtime arguing the point, Stingo changed the subject. 'Any news on Darcie?'

'No. The Russians are aware she might be in Jalabad and will look after her if she reaches them, but at the moment the war is too hot for them to try and find her. They say we can trust their man to stash her somewhere safe.'

'That's the best we can hope for, I suppose. I'll report in when we're ready to land.'

'Get some rest, Stingo. You've been on the go now for well over twenty-four hours. You'll be no good to Darcie with the reactions of a zombie.'

'Yeah, I will. Over and out.'

Petya's wife showed Darcie into the family's tiny bathroom where she had prepared a bowl of hot water and placed it in the shower cubicle. She pointed to the dry showerhead and shook her head, then pointed to the bowl. Darcie guessed that meant that normal water supplies were not functioning. On her way out, Leila patted a pile of towels and clothing.

'For Darcie,' she said, then closed the door.

Skin still sticky with Cornish seawater, Darcie relished the chance to clean up. Trying to be as careful as possible, she made sure she reserved enough water to shampoo her matted hair, using soap from a bottle that smelled of oranges. Once washed from head to toe and dried off, she turned her attention to the clothes.

Her own sat on the floor in a stiff pile, desperately in need of a wash. The alternatives were a colourful, fragrant cotton blouse, calf-length blue skirt and an embroidered belt with tiny bells. Putting them on, Darcie felt as if she was slotting into the country like a jigsaw piece that had finally found its place. Slicking a comb through her hair in front of the spotted mirror, she was surprised that her face did not look any different. She had been through so much in the last twenty-four hours and all she had to show for it was a cut on her temple and a few bruises.

Darcie emerged from the bathroom to find that Leila had set the table for a meal. She had lost track of time many hours ago so wasn't sure if it was lunch or dinner they were having. Babushka shuffled in and took the place at the head of the table. She nodded appreciatively at Darcie's change of clothes and mumbled something in Russian. Leila answered her with a few words that sounded like agreement. Leila served noodles deftly, on to their plates, then ladled on a sauce of lamb, peppers, tomato and onions. The three women sat together in companionable silence, each occupied with twisting the slippery noodles around their forks.

Unable to communicate, Darcie examined the furnishings of the room. A sofa bed stretched along one wall, covered in a scarlet and blue kilim throw. Like the hall, this room was a little museum of Tazbek culture – pictures of camel trains, oases, fragments of embroidered silk and polished silver harness buckles. It reminded her of the stories of the Arabian Nights, tales that never strayed far from the desert that lay just beyond the boundaries of exotic, many-towered cities. She caught an impression of people scattered across the great landmass of Asia connected by fragile threads such as the Silk Road to China.

Babushka Maria noticed Darcie's interest.

'My son,' she said with a mixture of pride and exasperation, 'he this.' She waved at the collection.

Leila excused herself from the table and returned with a photo of a man who had to be Petya's father. He had the same Genghis Khan looks, down to the moustache. Darcie brushed the edge of the much-handled picture with a respectful touch. A grandmother who lived in the Soviet era and a father who collected Tazbek mementoes; no wonder Petya called this a mixed-up country, she thought.

Babushka stabbed at the photo with a stubby fore- finger. 'Alexander. He teached Paschuk at University of Jalabad. Should shoot him, yes; no teached him.'

This answered the question of how Petya had been able to get so close to the general: Petya's father had taught Paschuk. It was a horrible position for Petya to be in, caught between loyalties old and new. Darcie knew enough about the collapse of the Soviet Union to understand that for the Tazbeks everything had been thrown into doubt; things that had once made sense, like the Lenin statue, now redundant.

Leila took the photo back and returned it to the other room before Babushka did any more damage to it. When she came back, she set about clearing the table, working silently around the black, boulder-like figure of Babushka who was murmuring away to herself in Russian, her face deep in shadows in the dim lighting. Darcie felt the atmosphere weighing heavily on her, a burden that she could not put down.

Suddenly the dusk was shattered by the wail of an air-raid siren. Darcie jumped. The Russians were attacking. What would happen now? They could hardly take her to a shelter with their inquisitive neighbours. To her surprise, both the women ignored the noise. The wail continued for five minutes then cut out. In the distance, Darcie could hear the rumble of what sounded like thunder.

'Bombs,' Babushka announced suddenly to the stillness. She pointed to the sofa, then to Darcie. 'Bed. Safe.'

'Thank you,' said Darcie. 'You've both been really kind.'

Babushka shuffled back to her lair and Leila retired for the night, leaving a faded nightdress, toothbrush and a quilt behind for their guest. A radio switched on in the next room, burbling away in incomprehensible languages interspersed with music. Darcie undressed and huddled under the quilt, counting the explosions until she drifted off into a fitful sleep.

Jalabad Palace, Tazbekistan: hot and sultry, 26°C

Paschuk had ordered that Carmen and Jake be held together in a room on the top floor of the old governor's palace – high enough to prevent escape out the window and with an unpleasantly close view of the bombing raids on the Tazbek television tower and local power plant. Carmen stood at the window, her fingers curled over the ledge as she witnessed the destruction of the Tazbek capital. Jake lay on a mattress, staring up at the beautiful, tiled ceiling. Centuries ago it had been decorated to look like the night sky – swirls of stars on a navy blue background – but patches of plaster now marred the picture where squares had fallen away. A new astronomical feature – 'white holes' – Carmen had quipped earlier when she had seen them.

Jake tried to feel grateful that she was attempting to bolster his spirits but it was too late. Seeing Darcie's body carried past him on the plane had been the final kick to his already flattened emotions. For the second time, he was going through the pain of losing her. He'd sunk far into himself, dealing with the death sentence hanging over his head by ignoring it and everything else. He knew that Carmen was worried about him, but mostly he couldn't bring himself to care. He felt three-quarters dead already.

The door opened and the guard with the walrus moustache who had executed Darcie entered. Anger flickered briefly in Jake's chest then went out like a match failing to catch.

'The general wants to see you both,' Petya said politely, bowing them to the door.

Jake did not move.

'Come on, my dear, our presence is required,' Carmen said with an admirable stab at brightness.

Still he did not get up. What was the point? If

they were going to execute him too, he might as well die lying down. He concentrated on the ceiling.

'Get up!' ordered Petya, injecting a little menace into his voice. He marched over to the bed and prodded Jake with the end of his gun. 'Now!'

'Or what? You'll shoot me? Not had enough of killing today?' Jake sneered at him, too bitter to care.

Carmen struggled to contain a sob, her hands over her mouth. 'Don't, Jake. Don't get them angry.'

'Doesn't make any difference what I do. Darcie did nothing – nothing but try to help and they killed her for it. He's going to shoot me anyway. Ask him.'

Petya lowered the gun. 'Do not be stupid. I will not kill you but you should listen to Madame Lopez. You have to come with us now.'

Jake turned his back on them.

Petya could feel his anger and frustration rising. The atmosphere in Paschuk's headquarters had felt odd ever since he got back from leaving Darcie at home. He couldn't afford to make any slip-up in the performance of his duties. He knelt beside Jake and shook him.

'You have to come.'

'Why?'

'Because you will make things much worse if you do not.'

'What do I care? You killed Darcie: I don't have to do anything you say.'

'I did not kill her,' Petya hissed. 'I only pretended to shoot her. I saved her from the crossfire and hid her on the plane.'

The boy still looked skeptical, suspecting another trick.

'Listen, she is now in my house being cared for by my family. She has courage, that girl. So now will you do what I ask?'

Jake turned slowly, unable to believe what he had just heard. He glanced at Carmen to see what she thought. The secretary general was hugging her arms to her sides, trying to warm herself with the one piece of good news they'd heard all day.

'Is this true?' Jake asked hoarsely.

'Yes, I swear it. Do not put me in the position where I am asked to choose between my duty and a child again. Get up.'

Jake rolled off the bed and stood. 'I'm . . . I'm sorry – and thank you.'

Petya frowned. 'Do not thank me yet. I may still have to make a different choice – one you and I will not like. Follow me.'

. . .

Paschuk received them in the throne room of the palace. The building long pre-dated the Russian power in this region, built for an almost forgotten khan who had ruled ancient Tazbekistan and much of her neighbours with his formidable nomadic cavalry. The chamber was a monument to that man's dominance: a ribbed azure dome like an inverted lotus flower, white kufic script rolling elegantly along the border where the dome met the supporting pillars, an intricate tiled floor that chilled the air. The windows were screened by carved wooden shutters. Carmen thought it looked all a little too perfect for its age – that was until she noticed the little plaque by the entrance extolling the Russian Ministry of Culture for its restoration of this jewel of the ancient Tazbek civilisation. Under normal circumstances she would have appreciated the irony that the Russians had provided the backdrop for another petty khan's ambitions, but for now she was feeling too anxious.

'Madame Lopez, I trust you are rested?' Paschuk asked from his seat behind a desk in the centre of the room. He had changed from his dress uniform to battle fatigues, a soft beret covering his shaved head. A computer screen and telephones sat on the leather surface, wires marring the patterned floor as they snaked to the wall sockets.

Carmen crossed her arms, wishing she were wearing something less frivolous than a red evening dress. 'Not rested, no. Just eager to find out what is next in your little drama, General. You've left murder and mayhem behind you in a neutral country, taken on the world by attacking the United Nations, and now got a war on your hands with one of the biggest military powers in the world. I shudder to think what else you have planned.'

Paschuk gave her a thin smile. 'Now you reopen negotiations, Secretary General.'

Carmen held his eye. 'For our release?'

'In return for recognition of Tazbek independence, withdrawal of Russian forces and a guarantee, underwritten by America, China and the European Union, that we will not be attacked.'

'You do not want much, do you?'

'I want what is owed to my people.' He gestured to a chair facing his own. 'Take a seat. There is another matter I need to deal with before we contact the Russian president.'

Carmen sat, crossing her ankles as she tried to make the flirty silk flamenco skirt behave. Out of the corner of her eye, she registered that Jake had moved to the side of the room, gravitating towards Petya whom they were both beginning to trust. 'Indeed? What matter?'

'The matter of the Russian spy in my camp.'

Years of diplomatic training enabled her to suppress her flinch. An obvious explanation for Petya's behaviour leapt to the front of her mind but she hid any sign of it. She prayed Jake would not give the game away by any untoward movement.

'Is that so, General? I would know nothing about that. As you are no doubt aware, the United Nations does not have its own intelligence agency. You could say we are more spied upon than spying.'

Paschuk stood up and resettled his leather belt more comfortably around his middle, flicking the buckle loose on his revolver holster. 'I did not say you would know; I merely wished you to be present while I explored my theory with my men.'

Wondering what trick Paschuk had up his sleeve now, Carmen folded her hands on her lap and kept her eyes fixed on her watch. She heard Paschuk get to his feet and begin patrolling the room, subjecting the men on guard to an intense inspection. He moved like a wolf trying to sniff out weakness in his pack.

'You see, Madame Lopez,' he continued from behind her in a deceptively conversational tone, 'I suspected that we had a traitor when the Russians strengthened the guard on the Goraty nuclear base two days ago. My suspicions turned to conviction when the English girl survived the dungeon.'

Carmen felt a flare of hope. 'You mean you've not been able to take the base?'

'Of course we have – but it was harder than antic-ipated and I am not –' he searched for the right word in English, clenching and unclenching his right fist '– pleased that we lost so many loyal men. I blamed one of my guard – a man called Mikhail Grudnov who failed to report in – but it appears he was dead all along.'

Paschuk strode to his computer and pivoted the screen so Carmen could see the BBC news front page reporting the two bodies removed from St Helen's – one British policeman and one terrorist.

'That means, Secretary General, that another of my men must be responsible for his death as he went missing many hours before the British sent in their joke of a rescue party.'

Carmen mentally cursed the world media for haemorrhaging information in an already critical situation. 'Are . . . are you sure? I mean, perhaps there is another explanation.'

'What? That the girl killed him?' Paschuk mocked.

'Or the young man – Hugo Kraus. He was with her. I think he survived too. Your man may have found them – they probably acted in self-defence.'

Paschuk frowned, his eyes skating across his guards again, few of whom were able to follow this discussion held in English. Petya kept his gaze fixed on a point just over Paschuk's shoulder, betraying not a flicker of interest in what was said.

Paschuk returned to prowling. 'That is a possibility. I had forgotten him. But what of the leak of information about my intentions? That cannot be explained so easily.'

Carmen shook her head. 'As I said, General, I have no knowledge of such things.'

'But I do. I have an instinct to sense when something does not fit.' Paschuk swung around. 'You, boy, why are you standing next to that man? You saw him carrying your friend's body after executing her.'

Jake quickly backed away from Petya but Paschuk's hand landed on his shoulder, stopping him in his tracks.

'You did not notice our friend Petya here? I would have thought his moustache would make him rather memorable. His father had one too, did he not,

Petya?' Paschuk switched to Russian. 'What would he think of you now, betraying your country?'

Petya swallowed and cleared his throat. 'You are wrong, General.' He still wasn't meeting Paschuk's eyes.

'Wrong? Wrong to attempt this coup, or wrong about you?' Paschuk put his hands on his hips. 'All right. For your father's sake, I will give you a chance to prove yourself. Shoot the boy.'

Petya's gaze swung to Paschuk's face to see if he was serious. 'What? Kill another child for you?'

'Did you? Did you really kill that girl?'

Petya nodded. 'Yes, sir. You saw me.'

'No, I saw you carry her body back to the plane. Why pick a body out of crossfire? Now I think of your excuses, they appear rather lame. And what exactly did you do with her when we landed? Why go to the trouble of burying her? I should have asked myself that when you made your request to stay behind in the midst of a crisis. Unfortunately another detail that slipped my attention – I am not pleased; I should know better than to let these things pass.'

Despite himself, Petya licked his lips, betraying his nervousness. 'I believed she deserved a proper burial.'

Paschuk waved the excuse away. 'That is no matter. Shoot the boy and prove your loyalty here and now.'

Glancing with dread across at Carmen, Petya took a step back and shouldered his weapon, aiming at Jake. Paschuk moved out of the line of fire.

'What the –!' exclaimed Jake, finding himself staring down the barrel of the gun.

'No!' shouted Carmen, rushing forward, but Paschuk grabbed her arm and hauled her back against his chest.

'Calm yourself, Madame Lopez. This is just something that has to be done.'

Sweat beaded on Petya's brow as he hesitated over taking the shot. The gun wavered. He would have swung it round on Paschuk and damned the consequences if the general did not have Carmen clamped in front of him.

'Please!' begged Jake.

Petya threw the gun aside in disgust. Two guards rushed forward and seized his arms.

'As I thought,' Paschuk said grimly. 'Take this traitor away for questioning. I need to know everything he has told the enemy. When you've wrung him dry, I'll dispose of him – personally.'

16

Petya's Apartment, Jalabad: temperature rising rapidly, 25°C

Awake when it was still dark outside, Darcie got up and tidied away her bedding. After days of living in danger, she was fed up of being pushed around by events rather than taking any initiative, but quite what she could do without jeopardising her new friends, she had no idea. Making the bed was the only thing she could think of and that made her feel even more pathetic. Petya was off trying to stop a nuclear war; Jake and Carmen were still held by a ruthless killer; and she was folding sheets.

When Leila came in with the breakfast, she found her guest sitting on the sofa. The little Tazbek woman chattered away, obviously enquiring over her night and how she was. Darcie nodded and forced a smile, but the whole performance felt fake. Leila was scared – nothing about this morning was normal despite the pretence that Darcie was a welcome addition to the household.

Over a breakfast of boiled rice, mixed with fried onions, carrots and raisins, Darcie mulled over her options, wishing for something that would allow her to take a little more control of things. She decided the least she could do was learn a few more words of Russian. It was no fun feeling a complete idiot not even being able to say 'please' and 'thank you'. Speaking slowly in simple English, Darcie managed to convey her request to Babushka Maria, who from the evidence of the glint in her brown eyes was delighted at being drafted in on such a worthwhile endeavour. Leila smiled fondly at the pair as she left for work, calling out something to the old lady, which made both the Tazbek women laugh.

Darcie raised her eyebrows quizzically.

'She say you new granddaughter for me,' explained Babushka. 'You make old woman happy. Make her useful.'

Darcie was rapidly warming to the old lady, seeing that the rather formidable exterior hid a soft centre. 'Where did you learn to speak English?' Darcie asked as she sharpened the blunt stub of a pencil Leila had found her.

Babushka thumped her chest proudly. 'During big war. I meeted British officer. I hear to radio. I speak good, yes? But many years no English – I forget much. You work hard and be as good as me in Russian, yes?'

Russian proved to be more difficult than anticipated. None of the other languages Darcie knew offered any help. The words felt like chunks of concrete in her mouth, impossible to chew and digest. An hour later, just as Darcie felt she had at long last got a handle on some basic phrases, a hammering on the front door interrupted their lesson. Darcie dropped her pencil in alarm, spilling paper all over the floor.

Babushka was already on her feet. 'Quick!' she said in Russian.

With instincts honed by years of survival under unpleasant regimes, Babushka pushed Darcie towards the bathroom. Snapping the door closed, Maria headed in the opposite direction to answer the summons. Shivering with nerves behind the shower curtain, Darcie heard the old woman grumbling and fumbling for the keys, delaying the moment when she would have to let their visitors in. The pounding continued. Darcie could think of no pleasant explanation for the aggressive demands being shouted from the landing outside the apartment. She realised that she had to hide more effectively than behind a flimsy curtain.

Slipping out of the bathroom, Darcie darted into Babushka Maria's room. This had a window at the back of the house, but how high up Darcie was not sure. Running past the shrine to Soviet greatness, she yanked back the curtain and swung open the thick double-glazed casement. There was a drop of about eight metres to the street below – easily far enough to break an ankle.

Voices echoed in the hallway, the shrill protests of Babushka answered by gruff demands. The crash of doors against walls confirmed that this was no neighbourly call. Darcie climbed on the radiator and on to the ledge. Just as she was steeling herself to make the drop, an army lorry swerved round the corner and drew up with a screech right under the window, parking the soft canvas top within reach – the raiding party a little late in trying to cut off all escape routes. Before the men jumped from the open-backed rear, Darcie dropped on to the taut canvas roof and lay flat, praying the outline of her body on the stiff camouflage would not be obvious to those inside the vehicle. Soldiers' feet thudded on the pavement as they disembarked, but no one shouted a challenge.

Darcie wondered how much time she had until one of the men searching the apartment looked out the window and saw her spread-eagled on top of the lorry. Surely not long? She wriggled to the gap between the canvas and driver's cab, then slid down, expecting any moment to be spotted. Still nothing. Peeking out, she saw the soldiers had fanned along the building, guns trained on all windows and doors. No one was watching the off-side of the lorry.

Hiding in plain sight – that was her best hope. Twitching her skirt and blouse straight, Darcie jumped lightly to the ground and began walking, intending to get off the street as soon as possible. Not far down the road was a baker's shop, blue striped awning billowing in the warm breeze. Passing within metres of the nearest soldier at a swift pace, Darcie pushed the door open and entered. A bell tinkled and everyone turned to look at her. The shop was crammed with customers taking shelter from the sudden influx of armed men outside. Normal business suspended, the owner was handing round cups of steaming tea and fresh black bread, a slightly hysterical holiday mood in the air. As a newcomer, Darcie found herself deluged with questions she could not follow. Guessing they were asking her what was happening outside, she resorted to the universal language of teenagers and answered with an 'I-don't-care' shrug. A couple of matrons tutted over her rudeness, but then ignored her, enjoying chewing over their own theories too much to worry about a stranger's lack of manners.

Darcie crouched against the wall in one corner, keeping an eye on events in the street while avoiding being drawn in to conversation. A piece of black bread and a teacup were pressed into her hand. She smiled her thanks up at the shopkeeper and whispered her newly learned Russian phrase for 'thank you', hoping her soft tone would disguise her accent. He nodded and retreated behind the counter to resume his position at the centre of the little storm of gossip and speculation.

Twenty minutes later, the soldiers outside piled back into the lorry and disappeared as suddenly as they had arrived. The bakery customers began to emerge cautiously on to the street. Darcie was eager to get away before someone tried to strike up a conversation. Putting the now empty cup down on the counter, she threaded through the crowd and walked off as if she had a definite destination in mind. Turning the corner at the end of the street, she cautiously made her way back to the front of the apartment building and ducked behind one of the cars parked haphazardly on the pavement.

From her position, she could see Babushka Maria standing in the communal courtyard being comforted by her neighbours, her stocky figure making two of her willow-thin elderly friends. Two soldiers stood on guard either side of the stairs up to the family home, watching the senior citizens with wary respect, while two more uniformed men emerged from the flat carrying boxes of papers. The old lady screeched with indignation when she spotted her picture of Lenin lodged precariously on top of the things being confiscated; she snatched it back and wagged her finger at the young man responsible. Neighbours joined in the chorus of condemnation and Darcie saw with satisfaction that Paschuk's men were shamed into handing over the sputnik and a box of medals. The soldiers loaded the remainder of the items into a lorry, climbed in and reversed out of the courtyard in a cloud of choking diesel fumes.

Babushka Maria did not retreat into the flat as Darcie expected. She continued to hold court, weeping noisily, waving her arms and exhorting her neighbours. They nodded in agreement, joining in like a modern-day Greek chorus. One elderly man disappeared and returned with a bunch of keys for an ancient flat-bed van parked in the yard. After a few words of encouragement from Babushka, the elderly ladies climbed painfully up into the back, mindful of their stockings and walking sticks. They then took seats on packing cases, Petya's grandmother in their midst. Darcie was torn as to what she should do now. She had no money, knew no one, could not speak the language. The only person who could help her was off on some mission with her neighbours. The van bumped its way slowly under the arch leading out to the road. Following her instincts, Darcie ran forward and jumped up on to the back just as it pulled away. Babushka shrieked with delight and hugged her to her bosom, chattering away in Russian to her friends. Darcie now recognized the word for 'granddaughter' repeated by each of the ladies. They pinched her cheek and lightly slapped her face as they congratulated Babushka on her new relation. Darcie had the distinct feeling from their shrewd expressions that they no more believed she was really the old lady's granddaughter than they believed she was Tazbek – an impression confirmed when one unwound her fringed scarf and wrapped it around Darcie's head, concealing her face. But wherever these women's loyalties lay, it was clearly not to Paschuk and did not involve handing over a girl to his thugs.

Darcie put her mouth close to Babushka's ear. 'What are we doing?' she asked.

'Petya,' the old woman replied, determination forged through the difficult days of the twentieth century glittering in her eyes. 'We save Petya.'

Jalabad Palace: storm approaching, 28°C

Jake sat on his mattress with his back to the wall, drumming out one of his favourite songs on his knees – the only way he could vent his frustration. After the incident where Petya had been exposed as a spy, Jake had been locked up alone in the tiled room. Carmen was required for the negotiations with Russia taking place in the throne room, but no one was paying attention to the British boy. Jake had spent the last few hours cursing himself for a fool. If only he hadn't stood next to Petya – if only he had been more convincing in his response to Paschuk's challenge! He was angry with himself for being such a wimp. Darcie had done all sorts of stuff – swum out of a flooded cell, set fire and water loose on St Helen's – and what had he done? Only damage.

And the next time that door opened and he was dragged before Paschuk, he was more than likely to end up dead.

He stopped drumming and the silence washed over him with a chill touch like a premature taste of death.

Tap, tap-tap. Tap, tap-tap. Jake forced himself to beat out a new rhythm, refusing to let the silence defeat him. Snatches of the best tracks in his music collection regrouped in his mind – powerful, don't-mess-with-me anthems – reoccupying the space he had surrendered to terror.

Like a mist lifting, Jake gradually realised that, faced with such a desperate future, he had nothing to lose. He didn't have to sit here waiting for the next thing to happen to him, he could take action.

Jake jumped to his feet. But what? His priority had to be to get out. He was only here to put pressure on Carmen; with him gone she would have more room to manoeuvre. If he escaped, he might be able to link up with Darcie and then they could get away together. Yet before he could even contemplate finding her, he had to save himself first. He already knew his room was too high up for him to climb out the window; the only way was through the door, which was locked and had a guard on the other side.

'Come on, come on,' he berated himself. 'There has to be something.'

He didn't think he'd stand a chance if he tried to attract the guard's attention then took him on. That was the 'straight-to-coffin-without-passing-go' card. But if he could make the guard think he had already escaped . . .

Rather impressed by his own brilliance, Jake studied the room afresh. Carmen's bed was a grand affair with canopy and high-sided frame. With its swathes of rose silk and gold painted ironwork, it reminded him of something out of Disney's Aladdin, but unfortunately without the genie. Could he climb on top? No, he would be too obvious. Underneath? That was a bit lame – it would be the first place the guard would check. Despite this, Jake lay on his stomach to have a look. What if he clung to the frame underneath, lifting himself off the floor: would there be a chance that the guard would not see him? It was worth a try. The worst that could happen was that he would be discovered and be back at square one.

Sliding under the bed, Jake got himself into position, ready to grip the frame when he heard the door open. Trying it a few times to get the hold right, he steeled himself for a long wait.

Stingo, Knife and Hugo drove into Jalabad in the disguise of Tazbek farmers. Having 'borrowed' a battered lorry from a farm out near the drop point, they had a cargo of apples in the back, hiding their small arsenal of weapons. With the rough cotton shirts over grimy baggy trousers, hair and skin darkened by a lavish application of mud, they looked the part of three impoverished peasants taking the desperate gamble of bringing their fruit to market even during the hostilities. With his guttural Russian, Stingo had had little difficulty persuading the soldiers at the checkpoints that he, his brother and his nephew (here he would slap Hugo on the back unnecessarily hard) posed no threat.

The other six men in the SAS squad had divided in half. Merlin, who was black, and two others, Tigger and Sven, had decided they couldn't pass as

Tazbeks so were posing as journalists for a satellite news channel – a useful cover for the comms equipment; the last three men had requisitioned a vehicle from an oil installation and were claiming to be foreign engineers. The plan was to regroup near the palace and distribute the smuggled weapons. After that there was the little matter of infiltrating Paschuk's head- quarters and springing Carmen and Jake before the Russians got there.

The squad arrived at the rendezvous on time, reporting no problems so far. Merlin had already scoped out the palace and come up with a plan to get in via the kitchen quarters. Hugo soon discovered his part in this was to wait outside 'on guard'.

'But I know Paschuk's men,' Hugo protested. 'I'm good with my weapon. I can help.'

Stingo gave him a disgusted look. 'Yeah, I know how good you are with guns. Stay outside and stay out of trouble. We need you here precisely because you know the faces. Your job is to watch if Paschuk or any of his men leave the building. Be alert in case they try and move the hostages – they must know the Russians are going to target the palace and will probably try to move headquarters to somewhere safer. We also want to hook up with the Russian agent, Petya, so raise me immediately if you see him. He's our key to recovering Darcie.'

Hugo listened to his orders with dismay. When he'd been sent on this mission with the squad he thought his dreams had come true and he'd get a chance to put his combat skills into practice. Instead he was on the subs bench. Swallowing his bitterness with difficulty, he nodded and took up his position in the cab of the lorry.

Stingo gave him a searching look. 'Stay where I put you or I'll kick your butt when we get out of here.'

'Yes, sir,' muttered Hugo.

Westminster, London: sunshine and showers, 17°C

Now that the crisis had moved to Jalabad, John Riddell was hosting a round table of all interested parties at the Foreign Office in London. The meeting included the Russian minister, Turgenov, the remnants of the Tazbek delegation, UN and American officials. So far it was a noisy and fruitless meeting of mutual recriminations. News that Rosa Mila had invited the SAS to rescue the hostages had not gone down well with Turgenov. He demanded a private word with Mila and marched her over to the antechamber where coffee was laid out on side tables. After five minutes of ranting, the big white-haired Russian warned the Tazbek leader that his army would not hold off their planned assault on the palace.

'We have to wrestle back control of the country, including the nuclear base, before Paschuk attempts to carry out one of his threats,' he told her in his hectoring tone. 'Consideration for the safety of the secretary general will only hold us off for a short time: I'm afraid that even Carmen Lopez weighs little in the balance against the safety of Moscow.'

'But, Minister –'

Turgenov refused to be interrupted. 'You know, Deputy Mila, that only the on-going battle for control of Goraty has saved her so far. Paschuk may claim to be in command of the nuclear missiles, but the truth is that his men are pinned down by our counter-attack. Nothing is entering or leaving the base; no warheads can be launched under these conditions. Until this battle is settled – and that will be by ground assault as none of us want to bomb a nuclear facility – we will take no decisive action against the palace.'

'Very good, minister,' Mila responded politely, reining in her temper. For all his bearish ways, she had come to realise during the siege that Turgenov was essentially a good man. 'It is fortunate in that case that our British allies are able to help us. You are obviously stretched thin with the fight for Goraty; you should be pleased they can deal with this secondary policing matter of releasing the hostages. As first minister of the Tazbek parliament I feel I have acted responsibly when I accepted their offer of assistance.'

Turgenov grimaced and drained his coffee cup. During the crisis he had learnt grudgingly to admire the Tazbek woman. She was intelligent and talked sense, her training as an economist allowing her to see the whole of a complex problem, rather than just the parts like idiots of Paschuk's ilk.

'And we do not need a diplomatic row with America's most important ally now,' Mila continued smoothly. 'It is vital that Paschuk is isolated, and that we, his enemies, do not quarrel among ourselves.'

'You are right, ma'am.' Turgenov gallantly kissed the back of her hand. 'This is a concession Russia is prepared to make to further our friendship.' Tucking her arm in his, he led her back into the conference room and nodded to Riddell. 'Give your men until dusk. If they can't get Madame Lopez and your boy out by then, they must withdraw. In any case, I want the SAS out of the country by midnight.'

'They have told me they will not need any more time than that,' Riddell assured him hastily. 'They only have one shot at making this succeed.'

'Good. See that they don't outstay their welcome.'

'And, minister,' added Mila. 'About the new Tazbek constitution – I assume that you are content for internal security matters to be my responsibility?'

Tugenov chuckled wearily, acknowledging the guts of the woman reopening negotiations in the midst of a crisis. 'I think we can come to an agreement on that, Deputy Mila.'

17

Jalabad Palace: storm about to break, 29°C

The flat-bed van carrying Darcie and the elderly women she had come to think of as 'The Grand- mothers' drew up to the front gates of the palace. A guard emerged to question the old man at the steering wheel, but Babushka Maria was having none of that. With Darcie's assistance, she clambered to the ground and berated the soldier herself, matching her five feet of determination against his six feet of puzzlement. Her demands grew shriller and shriller, gathering a small crowd.

'My grandson, son of Alexander Ilianovitch, you

have him. I demand to see him – and that general of yours,' Babushka announced, slapping him in the stomach with the back of her hand to reinforce her point.

'The general is very busy, ma'am,' tried the soldier.

'Busy? Busy?! I remember Yerdan Paschuk when he was a snotty-nosed boy who never washed his hands after using the bathroom!'

The Grandmothers wailed and shook their heads in condemnation.

'He is holding my grandson on some trumped-up charges – raided our home – removed the belongings of my Alexander –' Babushka Maria was winding herself up in to a real state, tears creeping down her wrinkled cheeks.

The crowd murmured angrily at the disrespect shown to the memory of one of Tazbekistan's most revered cultural experts.

The guard shifted his gun warily, wondering how to defuse the little round bomb of indignation fizzing before him. He couldn't possibly remove her by force – his own mother and grandmother would never forgive him if they heard of it.

'Please move along, ladies,' he said weakly. 'I'll

tell the general you were here. He is dealing with a crisis at the moment.'

'Crisis!' cried Babushka Maria. 'He created the crisis! The boy needs his head examined. He is like a drunk in charge of a car driving us all to ruin. Someone has to speak sense to him as you lot are clearly as foolish as he is! Let us through!'

Darcie, hanging back in the crowd, was not sure what was being said up front but suddenly the mass of people surged forward, pushing the hapless guard out of the way. Triumphantly, Babushka Maria and her cohort invaded the first courtyard to the palace, Darcie sliding along in her wake. She had no firm plans, other than a desire to help Petya, Carmen and Jake; but now she was in, she was willing to make it up as she went along.

The bolt drew back on the door. Heart thumping like a heavy bass guitar riff, Jake grabbed the iron struts and heaved himself off the floor, feet wedged painfully between mattress and frame. Footsteps and a greeting called out in Russian. Brief silence. A plate clattered to the floor as the guard swore. Blankets ripped off the beds, canopy pulled down – the soldier was frantic in his attempt to find the prisoner. Jake even caught a whiff of stale breath as the guard searched under the bed – and missed him in his panic. Jake felt a surge of satisfaction, mingled with terror: it was working! The man ran to the window and craned his head out, trying to work out just how the boy had managed to disappear. Seeing no trace on the ground below, he left the room at the double, calling for help to organise a search.

With a groan, Jake released his grip and dropped to the floor. Knowing that every second would count, he rolled from under the bed and staggered to his feet. Yes! Result! The guard had left the door wide open. Jake raced to the door and headed down the corridor in the opposite direction to that taken by the soldier. He did not know where he was going except that he had to descend two floors and then get over the wall. Piece of cake – or so he tried to tell himself.

Hugo sat hunched with his feet on the dashboard, hat pulled low over his eyes as he pretended to be asleep. In fact he was watching the guard get defeated by a small group of elderly protestors and their entourage of girls wrapped in headscarves and sympathetic mothers. 'Granny power,' he chuckled, as the posse moved into the palace courtyard, a swirl of colourful scarves and dresses against the backdrop of the soaring navy blue walls of the tiled archway entrance. The distraction was welcome news for the squad.

'Hey, chief, the good citizens of Jalabad are keeping Paschuk's men busy in the front courtyard,' Hugo reported to Stingo.

He received one tap back on the earpiece – the signal that the message had been received but that Stingo was not at liberty to respond. The squad would be inserting themselves into the building, aiming for the throne room where intelligence said that Carmen was being held.

Hugo went back to watching the drama, which had now moved within the gates. He would have almost missed the boy slipping out past the empty guard post if he hadn't been wearing a white waiter's jacket, much the worse for wear after its journey halfway across a continent.

'What the hell!' Hugo was out of the cab in a second and moved to intercept Jake. The boy was far too distinctive with his razored haircut and black skin – he had to get him under cover and quickly. Unfortunately, Jake had turned in the opposite direction and was now running down the first street leading away from the palace. Hugo picked up his pace, not daring to call out.

Hugo swore: Jake was going north. He didn't know it but he was heading straight for the frontline of this little war. Another block and he'd find his way barred by the gun emplacements and barricades of Tazbek soldiers.

As if to prove Hugo's point, a shell whistled overhead and slammed into a building two hundred metres away. The explosion brought glass lancing to the ground in a deadly shower. Hugo threw himself behind a car and covered his head. The Russian push to take the palace was about to start. Either that meant they had finished the job at Goraty or had lost the base and now had to take out Paschuk. Whatever the reason, this was one battle that no one would want to be caught in. Hugo leapt up, shaking the glass fragments from his baggy clothes. Jake was still on the pavement, a stunned look on his face as he wiped grit from his eyes.

Hugo reached him in six paces and hooked him by the arm. 'Yes, bud, you got it wrong. You're heading for the frontline.'

'Hugo?' Jake shook himself, wondering if he was hallucinating. Perhaps he was only dreaming that this rough-looking Tazbek had Hugo's face and voice?

'Yeah. The one and only.'

'What are you doing here?'

'Rescuing you. But hey, you get bonus points for escaping on your own. Serious respect, man.' Hugo shoved his ratty felt hat over Jake's head and began towing him back the way they had come.

'I'm not going back there!' protested Jake. 'I've got to get away.'

Hugo did not let up. 'Back there we have a lorry. Back there we have eight SAS guys. Back there I have a weapon. Just shut up a minute, will you? The Russians are about to drive their tanks down this street and I don't want to still be here when they do.'

Jake subsided as Hugo raised Stingo again on the wire.

'Sir, good news. Jake's out. Did it on his own. I'm going to stash him in the lorry.'

A single tap confirmed the message had been received.

'And, sir, the Russians are making their move. We don't have long.'

One tap, then three. That meant he should wait – they would need the lorry to extract Carmen.

Hugo shoved Jake quickly into the cab and

pushed him down into the footwell. He was prepared to follow Stingo's orders as he had been trained, but only until he saw the tanks rolling towards him. Then he was using his own initiative and getting them out of here with or without the rest of the squad.

'Stay out of sight. Guards are still busy with some granny protest but they will probably start wondering about us in a while. I may have to move the lorry if they do.' He made no mention of the tanks. No need to make the boy freak out.

Jake nodded.

Hugo stretched out on the seat, arm draped along the back, mouth open in a simulation of a snore.

'Help yourself to apples,' he muttered.

With a flick of a switch, the general broke off negotiations with Moscow and shook open the note his aide had passed him. He hadn't liked the Russians' attitude for the past hour – they seemed to be too confident, merely stalling for time with pointless bargaining over minor details of the deal he had asked Carmen to broker. Now the transmission was interrupted, the UN secretary general leaned forward, head on her arms, exhausted by the strain of the past two days.

Paschuk scanned the report. Petya Ilianovitch's grandmother and thirty other civilians in the front courtyard demanding to see him. News reporters sniffing around for a story. What did the general want to do?

He scrunched the report up in his fist. Could none of his men make decisions without him?

'Bring the old crone to me. Persuade the others to leave,' Paschuk ordered. 'I'll see her in the entrance hall.' He turned to Carmen, but she seemed to be either asleep or oblivious to what was going on. He jerked his head at the nearest guard, indicating that he was responsible for ensuring that the secretary general was still there when he got back, then strode from the room.

Carmen sat up slowly. This was the first time she had been left lightly guarded in an unsecured area. How could she take advantage of that fact? She eyed the soldier – it was the young man who had been with them in the study at St Helen's.

'What's your name?' she asked, giving him a charming smile.

The man stared right through her.

She repeated the question in her very shaky Russian. The only other phrase she had was that for 'cheers'.

He shook his head and raised his gun in warning.

Right, so the famous Carmen touch was not going to work with him. She threw away her last phrase at him.

'Cheers.' He looked confused. She held her hands out empty. 'That's it I'm afraid. I flunked Russian at diplomatic classes. Though I can say "cheers" in twenty-three world languages. Want to hear them?'

She didn't know if she was getting through, but she went ahead anyway. His eyes glinted as she reeled off German, Italian, Spanish and French salutations.

'Now it gets interesting,' she promised, moving to Portuguese, Hungarian, Finnish, Arabic, Amharic, and Cantonese.

The soldier actually cracked a smile. Good, he was thinking her a harmless old bird – that worked for her if flirting didn't.

She got up and stretched her arms above her head, continuing her litany of toasts as if her movement was entirely incidental. She paused by the window, wondering if she was close enough to the ground to risk a rapid exit that way.

'Now, Japanese, that's a real hard one. If I get the

intonation wrong, I might end up insulting your ancestors or something.' She clicked her fingers as if trying to remember and sidled to the ledge, perching one hip on the sill.

'*Nyet!*' barked the soldier, suddenly awake to what she was attempting to do. He hauled her back from the window and marched her to the chair. 'Not good lady. Stay there.'

Frustrated in her escape, Carmen stared straight into the guard's face and spat out a colourful curse learned in the slums of her childhood – something about gangrene and his manhood. He frowned at her, sensing her hostility.

I must be really losing it, thought Carmen wryly, wasting my best oaths on a hapless henchman.

'That's cheers in a local dialect in Bolivia,' she explained sweetly. 'You should try it next time you meet one of my countrymen.'

She had to content herself with the small satisfaction of leaving him with a rapid passport to a fist in the face; she obviously wasn't going to outwit him any other way.

Carmen froze. A dark-clad figure slipped from the shadows like a panther bounding in for the kill. Smoothly, he approached the soldier from behind and knocked him out, catching the body under the arms to lower him to the ground without a sound.

'Don't believe anything she tells you, mate,' said Stingo to the unconscious soldier. 'The lady has a filthy vocabulary.'

Carmen's eyes widened at his English. 'Who are you?'

'British. Friend of Darcie. Let's go.' He grabbed her arm and helped her to her feet. 'Any injuries?'

'No. But I can't just leave – not without Jake.'

'He's out already, ma'am.'

Carmen was still dragging her heels. 'But there's this other man – Petya. He helped us. He saved Darcie.'

Stingo paused. 'The Russian agent?'

'Yes – Paschuk guessed what he'd done and has taken him prisoner. He'll kill him.'

This wasn't in the plan – an extra rescue for someone held in another part of the palace, doubtless heavily guarded.

'Sorry, ma'am, but I am under orders to get you out. Once you are clear, I'll see what we can do for him. Until then, he'll just have to take his chances.' He didn't like to mention the fact that the palace was only minutes away from bombardment by Russian artillery.

'Jake's really out?'

'Yes, ma'am.'

Seeming to accept that this was the best she could hope for, Carmen gave no further resistance as Stingo led her towards the rest of the team. They emerged silently like shadows from their positions guarding the route that secured their exit through the rear of the building. In and out, leaving barely a trace but a few crumpled bodies and an absence where the secretary general had been: that was what they had been trained to do and it looked as if the mission had run perfectly.

'Yerdan, you give me my boy or there will be trouble!' Babushka Maria had worked herself up to a red-hot rage, losing all perspective on where she was. In her mind, Paschuk was a scab-kneed boy again and she the avenging grandmother. But Darcie, hovering to one side, had not lost her head: she could see that the little lady in the centre of the entrance hall standing toe to toe with Paschuk was about to be forcibly ejected. Good humour and respect for elders had its limits.

'Mrs Ilianova,' Paschuk said with crocodile smoothness, 'it is only because I respected your son

Alexander that I granted you this audience. Petya Ilianovitch is a traitor and a spy. He will be executed at dawn. Now take yourself home and stay there. If I see you again, I will not hesitate to eliminate the rest of the traitor's family – root and branch.' He nodded to two guards who stood either side of the little war veteran. 'Remove her.'

Darcie had seen enough. Babushka's pleas had failed and Petya was in serious trouble – fatal trouble if the merciless glint in the general's eye meant anything. Taking advantage of the fact that attention was on the indignant old lady cursing Paschuk, Darcie stepped back and slid into a doorway.

I must be mad, she thought, as she realised she had decided to go on a one-girl mission to save her friends. She opted to start with Petya as he was under the most imminent threat. Scared but determined, she watched from the shadows as Babushka was heaved outside, her legs kicking, thick support stockings wrinkling around her ankles as she hung between two soldiers. Paschuk barked an order to one of his guards, gesturing down a corridor on his left, then turned on his heel with military smartness to go back the way he had come. Following a hunch, Darcie decided to pursue the guard rather than Paschuk. With his mind full of Petya, it would be natural for the general to send someone to check up on him even if he didn't have time to go himself.

Counting to ten, Darcie waited for the hall to empty of men. She then ran lightly along the corridor, keeping to the walls and using all areas of cover – doorways, furniture – to hide from the guard she was following. He didn't appear to suspect her presence, not looking around once. The passage was hushed and smelt cloyingly of floor polish, reminding her of a museum with no visitors. The guard pushed through a heavy wooden door and proceeded down a bare corridor. Darcie took a chance, continuing the pursuit even though she would be exposed if he happened to look behind.

Reaching a bare chamber that appeared to have once been the servants' quarters, he paused and drew a key from his pocket. Overhead, the pale ochre plaster was crazed with cracks like eggshell after it has been crushed. The restoration project that had done such a splendid job on the entrance and front elevation of the palace obviously hadn't reached this end of the building yet. A chair and table, with remains of a meal scattered over its surface, were the only furnishing. Six heavy doors, set in opposite sides of the room in rows of three, led into small, cell-like rooms. The man peered through a grille into one of them. Satisfied, he then fitted the key in the lock and opened the door.

If Petya was in that cell, she would not have a better opportunity to free him. One guard only – and she had the element of surprise. Darcie looked round for a weapon, but all she could see was a bottle of vodka on the table left by the last man on guard duty. It would have to do. Grabbing it by the neck, she crept up to the door and peeked in.

Petya was curled in a ball in the corner, protecting his stomach. He had been badly beaten, his face swollen. The soldier was laughing cruelly about something as he prodded him with his rifle butt. Silently, Darcie glided up behind him and raised the bottle, praying this move would work as well as it did in the movies.

Crack! The bottle splintered and vodka spurted over both Darcie and the guard. It got in her eyes, stinging, blinding her. The guard cried out in pain, flailing around like a wounded bear. Not good. He was supposed to be down and out after that blow, but he was still on his feet. Before she could dodge out of his path, one hand caught Darcie by the throat and hauled her towards him. She could do nothing but scratch and kick – still incapacitated by her burning eyes. He backed her against the wall and his hand tightened. Panicked, Darcie tried to haul in a breath but could not; her struggles redoubled but she was weakening. She'd always known she wouldn't stand a chance in a fight against a fully grown man – had been told to avoid this type of confrontation – but it was too late now to go back and do it right. She gasped but no air got through the pressure on her throat. She was seconds from blacking out.

Suddenly the man jerked backwards and his grip loosened. He fell to the ground, dropping Darcie. She scrubbed her eyes, clearing her vision, to see Petya on his feet, stripping the guard of his weapon and securing his hands and feet with cloth ripped from his shirt.

'You all right?' he asked, his voice slurred by his split lip.

She nodded, trying not to cry after the shock of such a vicious burst of violence in a confined space.

A warm hand rested on her shoulder. 'Let me see.'

Darcie raised her chin so Petya could examine the bruises around her throat.

He gave her a lop-sided grin, a new gap where a tooth had once been. 'You'll live, little sister.'

'I think I'm in better shape than you,' she rasped.

'Are you OK?' She touched her hand gingerly to her neck.

Petya grimaced. 'Yes – and no.' He limped to the door, holding a protective hand over his ribs. 'Come, we must get you out of here. You should not have come.'

Darcie was stung that he appeared to be scolding her just after she'd mounted her rescue attempt. 'Yeah, you were doing so well on your own here, Petya,' she muttered sarcastically.

He swung round and favoured her with another grin. 'I did not say I was sorry to see you. You have the spirit of my grandmother – and that is saying something! I only meant that it is not safe to be here.' On cue, there came a percussive bang from some- where in the palace complex. Plaster that had hung on for centuries dropped in defeat all around them, dusting them with grit. Petya's manner shifted, like a speedway driver finding an extra gear. He grabbed Darcie's hand and began to run along the corridor leading back into the main part of the building. 'The bombardment has begun,' he shouted over his shoulder. 'That means the battle for the missile base has been settled.'

'Who won?' Darcie clutched at her throat; every word was painful.

'No idea. But it means I've run out of time; I cannot wait for orders. I must stop Paschuk before he has the chance to order a missile launch. My commanders have made plans for this moment. I must meet up with my comrades.'

Scooting along in his wake, Darcie felt like Esmeralda trailing the hunchback of Notre Dame: Petya's foot was dragging and he was bent over to protect his busted ribs.

'You're in no state to challenge him on your own!' she protested.

Petya wasn't going to be deterred from his mission. 'It is my job. If all goes well, I will not be alone. Get yourself out of here, Darcie. You have done more than enough and those shells will not know to miss you.' They had reached the entrance hall. He waved to the doors. 'Go!'

Darcie hovered, undecided for an instant. He was right: she could do no more here to help; but it didn't stop her hating the fact that she was watching Petya go off on what had to be a deadly task. Paschuk still had his men – still had the hostages as far as she knew.

'What about Carmen and Jake?' she called after him.

Petya shook his head. 'Just go. I will do what I

can for them.' He took a step back and gave her a little shove towards the door. 'The stakes are much higher than that, you understand?'

'All right.' She couldn't hold him up any longer. 'I'll go. Look after yourself, Petya.'

'I will – and thank you, Darcie, for getting me out. You are a true comrade.'

With a last wan smile, Darcie made her way cautiously to the front doors. Satisfied she was on her way to safety, Petya turned back in to the building to hunt down the general.

18

Jake got a jolt of surprise when Hugo suddenly sat up and reached for the ignition key, muttering curses as the lorry failed to start first time.

'What? Are the SAS here yet?'

'*Nyet*, comrade. But the Russians and their tanks are.'

Jake craned his neck over the dashboard enough to see three dull green tanks rumbling across the plaza in front of the palace.

'Market day is over for this apple farmer,' Hugo continued, turning the key again and this time being rewarded with a growl from the engine.

'Do you know how to drive?'

Hugo gave him an 'are-you-kidding?' look. 'Grew up on a farm, bud. What d'ya think?'

Jake shoved aside his irritation at Hugo's manner. 'Good – great. Just for the record, I don't, so don't go getting yourself shot or anything.'

'Didn't know you cared.' Hugo shoved the lorry into gear and reversed as fast as he could away from the plaza.

'Shouldn't you turn this thing around?'

'Shut up, OK? I'm the driver.' Hugo rammed the stick into first with a grate of the gears and swung the lorry round on a larger patch of clear ground.

'Stop!' shouted Jake, grabbing his arm.

'This isn't a freaking driving test, bud. I'm not doing an emergency stop in front of those tanks.'

'No, it's Darcie!'

Hugo followed Jake's finger and saw her on the front steps of the palace staring in astonishment at the three tanks targeted at her. The blue archway and bulbous towers reaching to the skies towered above her. The gun turrets swivelled towards her position like Daleks hell bent on extermination.

'Get out of there, idiot!' Hugo murmured.

They watched as Darcie dived back into the building just as the tanks let rip. Shells slammed into the delicate stonework of the palace frontage, reducing centuries of craftsmanship to rubble.

'We've got to get her.' Jake scrambled for the door.

Hugo grabbed his jacket, swerving to avoid a bollard. 'Forget it. She's toast – and we will be if we throw ourselves in front of the tanks.'

'We've got to tell the Russians who she is!'

'And how are we going to do that? Knock on those reinforced tin cans and ask for a quiet word? Leave it – if she has any sense, she'll find another way out.'

Hugo's wire screeched into life. 'Where the hell are you?' Stingo yelled.

'Two hundred metres from last position, sir,' Hugo reported, slamming on the brakes. 'Two hundred metres away from the freaking tanks, sir.'

'Stay where you are.'

Hugo kept the engine running as a party of nine people ran towards them. Seven jumped into the back as Carmen and Stingo slid into the front with Hugo and Jake.

'Get us out of here!' Stingo ordered as they heard another explosion from the palace.

Hugo put his foot down, making the tyres spin as the lorry sped away.

'No!' Jake shouted, grabbing Hugo's wrist as he

hauled himself off the floor and on to the seat. 'Darcie's still in the palace – we just saw her!'

Stingo went still. His expression sent shivers down Jake's spine it was so intense.

'Is this true? What's she doing in there?' Stingo asked, his voice ominously calm.

'We just saw her. She probably went in to save me and Carmen.' Jake wiped the back of his hand across his nose. His eyes were wet too. He hadn't realised till then that he was crying but he was too stressed to be ashamed. 'We've got to go back.' No way was he going to leave her to face the tanks alone.

Stingo's eyes went strangely blank as he looked from Jake to Carmen.

'I'm sorry, Jake, we can't go back.' His voice was almost robotic, drained of emotion. 'We had to evacuate by 1800 hours. The Russians have surrounded the palace now. It's my duty to get you and Ms Lopez to safety.'

'You can't just leave her!' Jake had lost it; he was yelling now. 'You're the SAS! You're supposed to help people in that kind of danger, aren't you?'

'Is there nothing you can do?' Carmen pleaded softly.

Sick to his stomach, Stingo shook his head. He

was living through his worst nightmare. 'All I can do is tell the Russians – not that that will make much difference. She's on her own.'

Jake clenched his fists and pounded Stingo's unrelenting chest.

'You – can't – just – leave – her!'

Stingo let Jake batter him, sympathizing with the teenager's fury. 'I have no choice, Jake. I'm under orders.'

'To hell with orders!'

Carmen studied the SAS man's rigid expression. His eyes were tormented even though his jaw was locked. 'Jake, please understand,' she said gently. 'He doesn't want to leave her any more than you do. He would go back if there was the smallest chance of getting through, but he can't. He's just had to make a terrible decision and you are not making it any easier for him.'

'I'm not here to make it easy.' Jake felt desperation welling up in him with every metre they drove away from the palace. He tried to clamber over Carmen and Stingo to reach the door. 'Let me out!'

Stingo pushed him back. 'Sit down, soldier,' he ordered in a voice that would put the fear of God into even the most rebellious recruits. 'You'll put us all at risk if you go haring off now. The Russian agent's still inside. He'll look after Darcie if he can.'

'Petya's no use – he's in a cell, probably half beaten to death by now! Stick this – I want out – let go of me.' Jake pushed Stingo's hand off his chest and tried to squirm past him.

Stingo lost his temper. He shoved Jake back in his seat. 'Listen, you can't have out. None of us can. I'd give my right arm to be able to ignore my orders – I would if I thought I could make a difference – but right now the Russian army is between us and Darcie. Got it?'

'He means she's a gonner, unless she gets very lucky,' quipped Hugo from the driver's seat.

'Shut up!' roared Stingo. 'Just drive.'

The force of the explosion had flung Darcie across the floor. She finished up in the stairwell. She crouched there, hands over her head, as stonework, glass and plaster clattered to the ground. A small fire had started up in the exposed beams of the ceiling, smoke curling along the rafters, caressing the old wood, wooing it to burn. She had to get away from here before the Russians sent another mortar crashing in to the front of the building.

Feeling dizzy, head still ringing from the boom of the explosion, Darcie found it difficult to think straight. She rubbed her forehead, aware of a crushing headache if she had time to stop and feel it. What now? She had at least one ally loose in the building – Petya – and in addition Carmen and Jake might be locked up somewhere, prey to the next hit. She should try and find Petya – he was her only hope if she wanted to rescue the others. Still shaky on her feet, she hauled herself over the fallen debris and climbed the stairs, following his last known steps. He had gone in search of Paschuk. If she found the general, chances were that she'd find Petya. She just had to make sure Paschuk didn't see her.

The doors to the throne room at the top of the flight of stairs had been blown open by the shelling. Darcie kept to the wall and peered round the door-jamb. Inside the room there was a flurry of activity – soldiers packing up equipment, others building barricades at the windows, sharpshooters in position to pick off any attack from the gardens. In the middle stood Paschuk listening with a thunderous expression as the young blue-eyed guard explained something to him. Then, with no announcement, the general drew his side arm and shot the man in the head. The guard dropped to the floor mid-excuse.

Darcie crammed herself back against the wall, swallowing the bile that had risen in her throat. When she next steeled herself to look, the body had been dragged to one side, leaving a red trail on the beautiful floor.

Paschuk beckoned an aide forward. The man came instantly, knowing better than to test the general when he was in such a murderous mood.

'Thanks to our late comrade-in-arms, we no longer have any hostages to negotiate with,' Paschuk said in a tone that suggested he was barely keeping a lid on his temper. 'All we have now is the control of the nuclear warheads.'

'But, General –'

He held up the hand holding the revolver, commanding immediate silence.

'The Russians do not think I have the guts to use them, but they are wrong. Give the order for an attack to be launched. Target: the Kremlin. Perhaps when their own palace is reduced to radioactive dust, they will take us seriously.'

The aide shook his head in disbelief. 'You can't mean – but, General, that will cause the death of millions of people – Moscow will be wiped out – the land a nuclear waste for thousands of years!'

'That's exactly what I mean. Do it!'

The man stood to attention. 'General, I have served you faithfully for ten years. I believe like you do in an independent Tazbekistan. I have proved by my actions that I would die for you. But this I can't do.'

Paschuk levelled the weapon between the man's eyes. 'Fine. In that case, die for me now.' The gun went off; the man crumpled – a second body to be dragged aside, but when Paschuk looked for someone to carry out his order, he found himself in a ring of hostile, disbelieving faces.

'My orders must be obeyed!' Paschuk roared, his face flushed red with rage, his grip on command and his own sanity slipping. 'If none of you will do as you are told, I'll do it myself!'

The men did not respectfully lower their eyes and go about their duties; they continued to stare. Paschuk felt the challenge to his authority.

He swept them with a contemptuous look. 'It seems I'm the only real man in Tazbekistan – the only one with the guts to do what is necessary!' He strode to the desk and picked up the phone. 'Get out, the lot of you! Go and save your own miserable skins!' He fired his gun at the ceiling, bringing a shower of plaster down upon himself, making his shaved head ghostly white. 'Go! Or I'll shoot you where you stand!'

Like rats leaving the sinking ship, the guards bolted for the doors at the far end of the room. Paschuk grabbed the phone from the desk and stabbed at the speed dial.

'Commander, your status?' he barked into the handset. He nodded once. 'I want you to redirect all manpower to enabling the launch of one SS-18. Target –'

His order was cut abruptly short as the line went dead. Swinging round he was astounded to see a girl standing against the wall with a bunch of cables in her hand. Their eyes met in a moment that seemed to last an eternity. Then, at the same instant, Darcie ran for the main door as Paschuk raised his revolver. A shot exploded a hairbreadth from her shoulder as she dived for cover. Rolling on to her stomach and flipping up to her feet, she half fell, half ran down the stairs, back to the shambles of the entrance hall. She could hear Paschuk in hot pursuit, anticipated a bullet in her back at any second, her only thought to hide. Two more shots missed her before Darcie tumbled off the stairs and crawled into the well that had protected her before – but it wasn't going to do the job this time – not with an enraged terrorist on her tail. She stopped, her back to the wall in all senses of the word.

Paschuk came round the corner and, seeing her trapped, slowed. He raised his gun.

'You are very irritating,' he hissed in English, his hand shaking in his fury. 'I kill you how many times? But always you come back. This time I do it myself – I do it so that you cannot return.'

Darcie closed her eyes, locking a whimper behind her clenched teeth.

Boom!

The entrance hall exploded – fragments of stone blasting horizontally across the room like cannon shot. A crack and snap overhead and rafters slammed to the ground. Grit peppering her skin like buckshot, Darcie curled into a ball, waiting for the fatal blow – but it didn't come. Gingerly, she opened her eyes. The place where General Paschuk had stood was now occupied by a cairn of stones jumbled with wooden stakes. The only structure left standing was the staircase she was under: the walls and roof had gone completely. Without leaving the building, she was now outside. Darcie remained crouched in her shelter, too afraid to move.

As the ringing in her ears faded, she heard a voice calling across the wasteland. 'Darcie? Darcie?'

She edged forward and saw Petya picking his way across the rubble, a squad of Russian soldiers behind him.

'Over here,' she replied, coughing on the dust still whirling in the air. Blood was trickling from the tiny scrapes left by the flying debris but she was amazed to see she had escaped major injury.

'Where's Paschuk?' Petya shouted, rushing towards her. He gripped her shoulders. 'I was leading my men into the throne room when I saw him run out after you – I was too late to stop him.'

Darcie pointed to the pile of stones. 'He's under there.'

Petya pulled her into a bear hug. 'Thank God you are alive.' He gestured to Paschuk's resting place. 'I hope one of those stakes went through the heart to make sure the old vampire cannot rise again.' Tucking her head under his chin protectively, he quickly explained to the Russian soldiers what she had told him and they started shifting the stones. No one was going to believe Paschuk was really gone until they had the body as proof. Darcie was just content to let someone else handle the aftermath, fearing that if Petya let go she'd probably just collapse in a heap like the building.

A shout indicated that the general had indeed

been found: crushed by the palace he had tried to take over.

'Come: we are no longer needed here,' Petya announced. 'I will take you with me for our debriefing – then we will see about getting you home. My grandmother and wife must be out of their minds with worry about you – as I was for a few moments there. I will say one thing for you, Darcie: you may be British, but at heart you are true Tazbek.'

'What about Carmen and Jake?' she asked shakily.

Petya laughed. 'They are safe, little sister. Saved by some friends of yours. A man who said his name was Stingo asked me to look after you. He said he was sorry they had to leave without you.'

'Stingo. That's great.' Darcie felt some of the tension in her relax. She hadn't known he was anywhere near but if he had Jake then that was good news. Everyone she cared about was safe. 'I need a drink – a cup of tea.' The dust had coated her tongue, making her mouth as dry as the desert. She was exhausted, bruised but otherwise in surprisingly good shape.

'We can fix that. Come.' Petya smiled. 'Tea – perhaps you are British after all.'

19

Brize Norton Airbase, Oxfordshire: cool and breezy, 13°C

The British prime minister, John Riddell and the Russian minister, Turgenov, waited at the front of the reception committee in the hangar to greet the secretary general as she descended from the RAF plane. To one side of the dignitaries, Mr and Mrs Bridges stood with their arms around each other, desperate to see their son. Carmen climbed down the steps leaning on Jake's arm, followed by a tired but jubilant squad. The secretary general was wearing borrowed army kit, having had enough of her House of Tsui evening dress to last a lifetime. Never again would she face down a kidnapper dressed like a flamenco dancer, she vowed.

'Secretary General, I can't tell you how relieved we are to see you in one piece!' exclaimed the prime minister.

Carmen delayed answering as she watched Jake being engulfed by a hug from his parents. She thoroughly approved as the family wept with relief and shouted with laughter.

Seeing all was well there, she approached the prime minister and shook his hand, murmuring appropriate thanks; she then moved on to kiss John Riddell on the cheek.

'How is James?' she asked.

'I'm delighted to say that he'll be all right. Out of intensive care, thank God.'

She squeezed his arm. 'Good.'

Turgenov greeted her Russian style with multiple kisses on each side of her face.

'My dear Secretary General.' He did not try and hide his emotion as his voice quavered. 'I am sincerely pleased that you survived and thank you from the bottom of my heart for your help averting a disaster of unimaginable consequences.'

'It was not me, Minister. You have an

extraordinary girl called Darcie Lock to thank for that.'

'But still, the peace talks could not have continued without you.'

Carmen smiled, her tiredness evaporating. 'So you are ready to go back to the table?'

'As soon as you are.' She rubbed her hands together. 'John?'

'Lead on, Carmen. I have a car outside for us. Deputy Mila and her delegation are already at the Foreign Office.'

'Well then, I think Tazbekistan should not have to wait any longer for a solution.'

Stingo watched the politicians file out of the hangar, not surprised that they had forgotten even to acknowledge the squad. Carmen had thanked them before they left the plane, but to the others the SAS's contribution was taken for granted; their role was to pull off the impossible then disappear from public view. But he didn't need thanks to know the squad had done a good job in Jalabad.

Seeing the black limos pulling away, Hugo threw his kitbag on the floor in disgust. 'That it?'

'What did you want?' asked Stingo. 'A pat on the head?'

Hugo shrugged. 'Dunno. Something – we almost died out there!'

Stingo rounded on him. 'No, you ran for your miserable life at the first sign of trouble, disobeying orders.' His angry tone was attracting the attention of the rest of the squad; they gathered closer to hear the altercation. 'The one who stuck it out was Darcie – she nearly lost her life. If someone should be getting the thanks, it's her.' Stingo didn't think he'd ever quite get over having to follow orders and leave her behind.

'Yeah, well.' Hugo flicked a wary glance at the other men.

'You need to take a serious look at yourself, Kraus. Your self-image and the reality are miles apart.'

A sports car pulled into the hangar, Mrs Smith at the wheel, face inscrutable behind sunglasses.

Hugo's relief was very apparent. 'Seems like my lift's arrived.'

Stingo shook his head in disgust. 'Nothing I've said has made a blind bit of difference to you, has it?'

'Nice working with you too, sir.' Hugo made his politeness sound mocking.

'You'd better hope our paths don't cross again, Kraus. And keep away from Darcie.'

'Tell her that.' Hugo jerked his head towards Mrs Smith. 'I can't help it if the boss has other ideas.'

'For your own sake, you'd better find a way. It's not just me, but every man in this squad who'll be after you if you don't.'

The men muttered their agreement.

'See yourselves as Darcie's protectors, do you?' Hugo couldn't resist a sneer. 'Looks to me she doesn't need you.'

'Yeah, she's one of a kind, isn't she?' Stingo smiled, showing just a hint of teeth. 'Need us or not – we're here for her. And don't you forget it.'

Jalabad Airport: sunny, chance of showers later, 25°C

The ancient flatbed truck bumped along the road to the airfield with its cargo of elderly Tazbeks, a Russian agent and a Western girl. Darcie had opted to stand holding on to the side in an attempt to cushion the journey with her own balance, rather than have her spine rearranged by the jolts in and out of the potholes left by the recent mortar attacks. Babushka Maria and friends bore the discomfort with resignation, only breaking in to ululations of disapproval at the worst of the bumps.

With the wind whipping through her tangled black hair, Darcie took a final opportunity to admire the Tazbek countryside. Navy hills fringed the flat plain like a jagged frill round a tray-bake cake. The blue sky looked as if it had been dusted with icing sugar as the clouds were so high, wisps and swirls across the quiet expanse. No puffs of smoke or thunder of explosions marred the peace. The conflict had swiftly wound down with the death of General Paschuk; the nuclear base had surrendered to the Russian commander and the final pockets of resistance had been eliminated. Twenty-four hours later, Deputy Rosa Mila returned to her shell of a palace in the company of Minister Turgenov. A fresh round of talks had been scheduled for the following month, Carmen once more in the chair, her passion for Tazbek peace undimmed despite, or maybe because of, her recent experiences. The Russians had promised to restore the palace they had destroyed to its former glory (again) and the Tazbek government had moved in to temporary quarters in a nearby school. Tazbeks were joking with their customary black humour that the second wave of the Russian invasion would be its construction teams, with their body armour of hard hats and day-glo vests.

'Job creation,' Babushka's neighbours had joked. 'Bomb the hell out of a country then go in to rebuild it.'

Darcie scanned the airfield as they drew nearer. Petya had not been certain how she was going to be extracted from the country; only that his Russian handlers had promised to look after her and make the arrangements. Her heart lifted when she spotted the NATO helicopter – a Chinook – waiting on the tarmac. They hadn't let her down. She really was going home.

She couldn't wait to see her parents, tell Stingo her news, compare notes with Jake. What would the other pupils in her class in Truro make of their adventure? Dare she say anything? Darcie laughed: at least she wasn't alone this time. Jake would be with her, spinning the same tales of international espionage and danger. And there was still the little matter of that date they had arranged . . .

The van drove unchallenged through the perimeter gates and all the way up to the helicopter before coming to a stop. Darcie jumped down and helped the ladies out. One by one the Grandmothers hugged and kissed her, pressing little gifts of embroidered scarves, beaded bags and homemade biscuits in her hand. Last of all, Babushka squeezed her tight to her ample frame and then placed a medal in Darcie's hand. It hung from a red ribbon, edged in yellow, and was engraved with a picture of her hero.

'Darcie, good, strong. Like Maria.' She tapped her chest. 'You have my medal. Order of Lenin, first class.'

Darcie felt too choked to say anything. She pinned the medal to her blouse, then kissed the old lady on the cheek.

Babushka patted her face gently. 'You good girl. Stay safe.'

Darcie turned to face the helicopter and Petya standing between her and the open doors.

'Comrade. It has been an honour serving with you,' said Petya, saluting, then gathering her in a bearlike embrace.

'You'll be all right?' Darcie asked, her question a little muffled from the midst of the hug.

'Yes, yes. My wife and I, we go to Moscow – Babushka too. They have offered me a job there. Not all my neighbours liked what I did so it is best we leave. And you?' He sounded brave rather than pleased; Darcie doubted that he really wanted to go into exile away from the country he loved. But there was nothing either of them could do.

Darcie laughed softly. 'Back to school.' She couldn't believe how wonderful that sounded. 'I've got so much to catch up on.'

'But at least you can find Tazbekistan on the map, no? Not like other ignorant British children.'

'Yes, I can find it – and I won't forget it. Thanks for everything.'

With a final hug, they parted.

'Keep out of trouble, little sister!' called Petya, waving as she accepted a hand from the airman inside the Chinook.

She waved back. 'I'm counting on it!'

The crewman relieved her of her bag and presents then showed her to her seat up front. The whine of the engines signalled they were about to depart.

'Buckle up and make yourself comfortable, kid. It's about a two hour flight to our base,' explained the crewman. 'Can I fix you a drink? Coke? Root beer?'

Darcie felt her smile slowly fade. 'You're American.'

'That's right. The Russians asked Uncle Sam to come fetch you.'

Her heart slammed in her chest. Don't panic,

Darcie told herself. This might mean nothing at all. After everything that had happened, the Americans wouldn't be worrying about her undermining the president's re-election campaign, would they?

'Where's my mum and dad? Are they meeting me?'

He shrugged. 'Sorry, I don't know nothing about that. All I know is that the president himself asked us to pick you up real quiet, make you feel like a VIP. He's taking a personal interest in your case. You're one lucky girl.'

The helicopter took off and circled the airfield. The Tazbek party covered their faces with their scarves against the swirling dust. Too late to go back now.

'I'm lucky?'

'You sure are, kid. President Morris said we should treat you nice. So sit back: there's nothing at all to worry about.'

ABOUT THE AUTHOR

Julia Golding is a multi-award winning writer for children and young adults. Former British diplomat and Oxfam policy adviser, she has now published over fifty books in genres ranging from historical adventure to fantasy.

Along the way, between having three children, she took a doctorate in English literature from Oxford. Her first novel, 'The Diamond of Drury Lane' (2006), won the Waterstones Children's Book Prize and the Nestle Children's Book Prize. In the US, 'Secret of the Sirens' won the honor book medal of the Green Earth Book Award.

For more information visit
www.juliagolding.co.uk

ALSO BY JULIA GOLDING

The Companions Quartet

Secret of the Sirens

The Gorgon's Gaze

Mines of the Minotaur

The Chimera's Curse

Young Knights of the Round Table Trilogy

Young Knights of the Round Table

Pendragon

Merlin

Mel Foster Series

Mel Foster and the Demon Butler

Mel Foster and the Time Machine

The Cat Royal Series

The Diamond of Drury Lane

Cat Among the Pigeons

Den of Thieves

Cat O'Nine Tails

Black Heart of Jamaica

Cat's Cradle

The Curious Crime

Dragonfly

The Glass Swallow

The Ship Between the Worlds

Wolf Cry

Printed in Great
Britain
by Amazon